# Shield the Joyous

*For Maggie —*
*So great to read with you in*
*G'boro! And I love your work!*
*With gratitude,*
*Chad*

*Nov. 7, 2024*

# Shield the Joyous

a novel by

## CHAD HOLLEY

BULL CITY BOOKS

Durham, North Carolina | 2024

Parts of this novel have appeared in earlier form in
*Saint Katherine Review*, *Cloud 9 Magazine*, and *storySouth*.
Grateful acknowledgment is made to these publications.

Designed by Dave Wofford of Horse & Buggy Press
Printed in Canada by Friesens

Published in the United States of America by
Bull City Books LLC
PO Box 2817, Durham, NC 27715
bullcitybooks@gmail.com

For more information or to purchase additional copies:
bullcitybooks.com or chadholley.com

First Edition

For Claire, Jack, and Nate

Centuries of centuries and only in the present do things happen; countless men in the air, on the face of the earth and the sea, and all that really is happening is happening to me . . . .

—Jorge Luis Borges, "The Garden of Forking Paths"

Art and morals are . . . one. Their essence is the same. The essence of both of them is love. Love is the perception of individuals. Love is the extremely difficult realisation that something other than oneself is real.

—Iris Murdoch, "The Sublime and the Good"

# God's Possum

ZEKE BARRY lived up the big hill at the back of the neighborhood, and for several years his mother had given me a ride to school of a morning. Zeke and I were in the same grade, his sister Wendy in the one ahead, and Mrs. Barry managed the tellers at the downtown bank. So at ten minutes after seven, in all weathers, the Barrys' long, butter-colored Oldsmobile would pull up in our driveway, under my basketball goal, to sit and wait for me. (None of our mothers were honkers.) The morning sky seemed always to cast an impenetrable glare over the windshield as I walked out of our carport, around to my rear passenger door, to climb into the back seat beside Zeke.

If Wendy never once, to my recollection, turned around from the front seat to speak to me, this felt more to do with modesty than rudeness. Of course, Zeke and I didn't speak, not at this hour, not in front of his mother and sister. Mrs. Barry alone spoke, with a polite half-turn of her shoulders, a distinctly bovine roll of her eyes toward the back seat. "Good morning, Michael." "Good morning," I said. And we were off. Only: sometimes I would climb in beside Zeke to discover the passenger seat in front of me was empty—no head there, no shoulders, no luxuriant brown curls cascading down the seatback—and by the time I started seventh grade, I sorely resented the effect this had on the remainder of the ride, the energy it sucked out of it.

What had Wendy Barry done to encourage me? Little, in fact. Though she displayed none of the contempt one ought to expect from a pal's year-older sister, the only nip of flirting she had ever indulged me was an unforgettable chase through the Activities Building at First Baptist a year or so before. It was one of those spectacular, pre-adolescent frenzies that involved long hallways, a couple of stairwells, and a gaggle of other kids. But rising to something in the occasion that surprised us both, I think, I had eyes and legs and lungs only for her, and in the manner of her flight, her flapping and shrieking, she made evident she'd noticed this and did not mind, which drove me on, against the burning in my legs and chest, the rattle of thickened saliva in my throat, until at last Wendy led us, alone, flying down the gallery that overlooked an indoor basketball court, where at the end of the passage, with but two strides between us, she went slamming—*blam!*—through the girls' bathroom door. I braked instinctively. I had not seen this coming. For a moment I stood staring at myself in the push-plate of perhaps the most sacred boundary I knew, scarcely able to imagine the country beyond. And before I had decided what I would do, my name came booming up through the building in a husky timbre I have never forgotten— MY-KUHHL!—and I looked down upon the basketball court to find Wendy Barry's father, a stout man with a graying cannonball for a head, sitting in a metal folding chair behind a spread-open newspaper, eyeing me sternly over the top of his reading glasses.

I will not say that but for this moment I would have made a different kind of citizen. But I do believe it gave me, from early on, a certain empathy with those against whom the shepherds of the earth practice all their vigilance. Less prospectively, I gazed at my feet on the carpet of the second-floor gallery of the Activities Building of First Baptist, appalled to the point of nausea at my clumsiness, my simple and utter circumscription. And turning without a word, I gave them that bathroom door.

How I asked Wendy Barry to Go with me still embarrasses me. It is one of those things I have done (oh, that list) that I'd have liked to suppose was beneath me. But then seventh grade—junior high!—had rather gone to my head. And one afternoon that first week, sitting in the tropical, postprandial heat of an exceedingly gradual course in Pre-Algebra, I decided that when the bell rang I would get up from my desk, wade out amid the torrent of faces in the hallway, find Wendy Barry, and without the faintest warm-up to the subject, blurt: "Hey, baby, Go with me." The salutation, the racy use of the imperative, they were without question the influence of Arthur Fonzarelli. Nevertheless, it was I who chose them, and when the bell had rung and I had drifted up alongside Wendy Barry in the hallway as planned, it was I who delivered them.

The girl did not break stride, but gawked without reserve.

"Oh, my gosh," she said.

Upon which, in the crush, we were parted.

Wendy still wore braces on her top and bottom teeth, but the rubber bands were gone, her complexion was clean, and she had big hair. Meaning, I understood she did not lack for suitors. Even a boy in the high school, I'd heard, had signaled some interest, notwithstanding this was one Greg Randolph, a cocky, rope-chain-over-turtleneck tenth-grader who was over-proud of his driver's license and a part-time job at the hospital that let him wear scrubs. Plus I'd pretty well accomplished all I'd envisioned to this point. So while being made to wait the rest of the school day for an answer was tedious, I did not begrudge it. And I was beatboxing in my bus line, the creme filling in a group that called ourselves the Oreos, when Wendy's best friend, the imperious Head Rifle of our marching band (whose imperious mother gave Zeke and Wendy a ride home in the afternoons), walked up and waited until she had my attention, which was not long:

"Wendy says okay."

Maybe a shade less affirmative than I'd hoped for, but in fairness there was no actual question pending, and in truth I did not take it amiss. What perplexed me was what followed. Namely, that despite complying with my best guess at what to do when a girl agrees to Go with you by walking straight to her house after school, I could pry no further word from Wendy. She was down the Barrys' long hallway, in her bedroom, with the door closed. I was in their living room, watching a PG war movie on HBO with Zeke, who refused to make inquiries on my behalf. "She ain't talking to me," he said, returning from his only attempt, "—oh, watch how far he throws this hanger-nade." Likely I would have admitted being responsible for a certain vagueness in Wendy's and my new arrangement. I might even have admitted her coming out and joining me on the living room sofa was only going to present new and more urgent quandaries. But I couldn't take this anymore, these hushed, lamplit rooms, the chattering television, the ear-splitting aria of awkwardness, confusion, tension.

I said, "Let's go outside."

IN THE YARD about the Barrys' house the air was thrumming with bugs and heat, the day was more intelligible. Here I knew what I was about. We shot a squirrel out of the top of a pine tree with a .410 Zeke brought out of the house with us for that purpose. I had my misgivings, but he said his daddy had told him it was okay—the squirrels had been tearing up their bird feeders—and besides it was an admirable shot. (Which imparted a new respect for Zeke, as he was not much of a student or trombonist and ran funny.) The immediately dead squirrel made its way down through the limbs and pine needles like a prop in a skit and whumped on the grass at our feet. Needles went on raining after. We picked up the squirrel and studied it, still quite warm and loose-jointed inside its fur, and on the whole rather less disfigured by the little shotgun than we expected. We discarded it.

We had not come out to hunt squirrels, but the activity

seemed to have chosen us. We peered into the tops of other pine trees in the Barrys' yard, staked out the live oak in front. Huh. No more squirrels.

We retired the shotgun and set a medium-size gasoline fire on the concrete patio behind the Barrys' house. We threw newspaper on it to keep it going, but then orange and black newspaper ghosts began to rise up out of the flames and float off into other yards, into the shrubs and carports of other houses, which seemed dangerous. We stomped the flames flat, scuffed the ashes over the scorched concrete.

We descended the viny ravine off the back patio and found half a can of black spray paint buried in the kudzu. We uncapped the can, sprayed it empty, and began to slam it against the trunks of trees to get at the little ball we could hear rolling and plinking around inside. It had become an object of intense speculation. What did it look like? How big was it? What was it made of? How did they get it in there? And how come you never heard anybody talk about them? I mean, they were sort of an obvious thing, weren't they, all the millions of cans of spray paint out there and a little secret ball of some kind clattering around in every one?

Aerosol paint cans, turns out, are tough. We took ours back up to Zeke's house, to the woodpile beside the patio. Zeke went around the front of the house, to the tool closet in the carport, and came back with his daddy's axe. We took turns with it, but the paint can just kept spinning and skittering around on the surface of the chop stump.

I said, "Get down there and hold it."

He said, "You get down there and hold it."

It was his house.

I knelt in the chips. I reached out on the stump and put a hand on the can. After a second I thought better of this. What we had here was one stubborn paint can. I took hold of the can with both hands, one at each end, like I was measuring how long it was. "Let her rip," I said, and brought my chin down onto the stump, for the excellent view.

I do not remember hearing Zeke give any warning. I do not remember being aware he had even lifted the axe. I remember only the sudden, dark veil, the rolling away from the stump, the staggering about, the screaming, and the slow, dazed inference, upon re-opening my eyes, that I probably looked a lot like Zeke did. Which is to say, black. For an empty paint can, this one sure had a lot yet to offer.

We tore the ball out of the wrecked can and looked at it—in the light of day it was just a smeary plastic ball, the size of a penny gumball—and we slung it pattering down through the leaves in the ravine. We had stopped moving around in that careful way you do when coated in a foreign substance, but among other inconveniences our hands were slicked to the point it was hard to hold things, and I for one was needing to resume normal manual activities, like tugging at my crotch.

Gasoline cuts paint. We still had a whole coffee can of good gasoline. So we poured gas over our hands and arms, splashed it in our faces, rubbed it in our necks like aftershave. We damped each other's hair with it and picked out the gummy, bug-like beads. We cleaned the head of his daddy's axe, wiped down the handle, sloshed gas across the surface of the chop stump. We and our vicinity were now a pallid gray and the air about us was thick with squiggly lines.

I said, "Wonder if Wendy's come out yet."

He said, "I doubt it."

We went back inside to see. The TV was still on, but no one was watching it. The rooms were still quiet and lamplit. The air was still thick with squiggly lines.

"Told you," he said.

We stood around the fireplace in their living room for a few minutes lighting matches and throwing them at each other.

Then I said come on, and started back outside.

Zeke said, "Where we going?"

I said, "First, we need a shovel."

THERE WAS A VACANT LOT beside my house, the better part of it thickly wooded and caney. And deep within that part, in a sanctum-like clearing, stood a rotted-treehouse tree where I had a three-days-dead possum lashed to the trunk with a nylon rope, high enough my little sister and brother and the neighborhood dogs couldn't get to it.

There is so much I want to say about this possum that my heart aches with the effort, and I hardly know where to begin. Over the years I've recalled it, revisited it far more than most people I've known. Too often it's overlooked that a considerable portion of a life may be lived in the dreams and memories of others. Let's say, then, I speak here of an uncommonly old possum, in peculiarly good health.

My father shot it in our back yard, constructive gunfire being a not infrequent occurrence in the neighborhood. Our highstrung Irish Setter, Lady, had cornered it against the wooden fence near our trash cans, and my father didn't want Lady fighting it and getting rabies. So he chose a little .22 rifle out of our gun cabinet, shot the possum, and pitched it over the fence, into the high, thick greenery of the vacant lot.

It was not hard to find. It lay grimacing in a cloud of loud flies amid the cane. I carried it by the cord tail up to the clearing around the rotted-treehouse tree and laid it on the dirt. I knew I was on shaky ground, having started junior high, but I petted the possum on the fur and spoke to it. Nothing looney, just a simple, but odd-feeling, "Hey, possum." And somehow, saying the words out loud like that made the possum lying there on the ground seem especially still and dead, and the moment all around me in the clearing seem very big and tingly, so that I marveled at the size of the moment, and responding to some throbbing compulsion in it, I ached to expand to match it, to take the whole of it inside me, to leave none of it outside me, and at the same time suffered a distressing certainty that I could not, that by some cruel, indefatigable math this was not possible, a moment is not containable. The effect of it all was that I thought I might cry, and I was willing, and waited, but no tears came. It occurred to me this might be because I was in junior high. I tied the possum up on the tree to leave it.

And I saw something.

From the exposed belly of the dead possum, there was hanging a little gray string.

It seemed like the kind of thing you might not ought to pull on.

I pulled four little wet-looking dead baby possums out of the one hanging on the tree. They made the air in the clearing ring with a high-pitched silence while I sat on the dirt and twigs and studied them. But even as a grown man I wouldn't know what to do with such a gift as I felt had been bestowed on me, and I think I ended by pitching them gently over into the cane.

When Zeke and I reached the vacant lot beside my house, I led him into the quiet, dirt-floor room amid the vine and foliage. I showed him the possum hanging on the tree. He liked it. I could not find the babies in the cane, but we took a pair of small sticks and found two more baby possums inside the one hanging on the tree. Then we took the big dead possum down from the tree, put it together with the two new babies in a garbage bag, and pressed the extra air out, like you do for the last two or three pieces of a loaf of bread. The bag blew its tart, three-days-dead-possum breath in our faces.

We buried the bag of possums down the street, in John Dixon Montgomery's mother's vegetable garden. A choice motivated by our memory of how the Indians had shown the pilgrims how to drop little dead fishes in their seed holes and how that had led to cornucopia and Thanksgiving. It pleased us to think the possums would become the earth, the earth would become tomatoes, squash, watermelons, and okra, the tomatoes, squash, and okra would become our parents, the watermelon us. We spoke of this as we refilled the hole, over the sound of dirt hitting black plastic garbage bag.

Afterward we went dragging the shovel up the street (for the sparks) under a sky that was high and mild, beneath a cool and distant sun, and all around us, throughout the neighborhood, yellow and red and purple leaves were raining from the trees. It was one of those times when the world is so exquisitely beautiful you are convinced we are, each of us, ultimately alone. And on reaching the big hill that led to Zeke's house I glimpsed, in the woods that edged the street there, the tall and balding figure of Ol' Cletus, our sad-case inhabitant of the grimy little house tucked among cedars over at the Angel's Pond. From the corner of my eye I watched him slip from trunk to trunk through the falling leaves, keeping pace with us, but did not mention it to Zeke. First, I believe, because I dreaded the disruption this odd visit might bring, particularly should our parents hear of it. Also because, when I risked turning my head for a better look at the man, every space amid the trees stood empty.

We stomped our feet on the mat at Zeke's house and went inside. It was still quiet and lamplit. It still smelled like gas. Down the hallway, Wendy's door was still shut.

We ate a bag of microwave popcorn out of a china bowl. I wished my mother would buy this stuff, but my father wouldn't have it, on the grounds they'd not yet figured out how to make it so most of the kernels popped, it was wasteful. By contrast, we ran through boxes of microwave pancakes. When Zeke and I finished the popcorn, I called his attention to the large number of unpopped kernels in the bottom of our bowl. He didn't appear to share my father's concern.

The phone rang. Zeke sucked his fingers clean and answered it. He said, "Yes, ma'am," and with someone's voice still humming in the receiver, handed it to me.

It was John Dixon's mother. She wanted to know what was in the bag she'd seen us burying in her garden. The dog had dug it up and was dragging it around the backyard, and it stunk so bad she was afraid to look in it.

I said possums.

She said okay, well, would we please come get it.

I said yes, ma'am, we would.

I hung up the phone, and we set off down the street, carrying a hammer and nails.

SURE ENOUGH, John Dixon's dog had dragged the garbage bag around their yard and ripped it up. We couldn't find the two baby possums.

We let John Dixon's dog have what was left of the garbage bag and walked out the back of the yard carrying the big dead possum upside-down by the tail and a hammer and nails. We followed a dirt path into the trees, wound through a rolling gray fog of brittle briars, a private dump of coke bottles and oil filters, banks of blossomless honeysuckle. The path then turned down into the ravine, through loose rock and hardwoods, where midway down we paused—to hear the purling of the creek.

No boy among us knew a more constant friend. Meandering through the middle of the neighborhood, our creek occasioned the superb concrete, guardrailed bridge in the street near my house, but as a rule contrived to show itself to adults only there. Everywhere else the creek kept to the woods, beyond the ken of the streets and yards and houses. We never found where the water in it came from—it skirted the Angel's Pond, without joining it, maybe a mile upstream—and we never knew where it ended, though we had walked it whole days in both directions. Singly, in pairs, in troops, we splashed along its gravel shallows, shucked our shirts and shoes to slither down its marbled clay banks, waded its black, neck-deep pools, daring ourselves toward some dark den amid the gnarled roots at the waterline. We had stoned and stabbed at snakes beyond number in the creek. We had fished up crawdads the size of small lobsters, using rod-and-reels baited with ribbons of raw bacon. Some of these crawdads were a winey red, and some a translucent, exoskeletal gray, and some had beautifully colored pincer-tips, bright black and red and yellow, like the beaks of tropical birds. It was, our creek, the very animating principle of the neighborhood. And not incidentally, I suspect, do I remember walking it only once with an adult.

IT IS A VAGUE but affecting memory. We have just moved into the neighborhood, my father and mother and I, and my father has laced on the olive-green combat boots he brought back from Vietnam, and he has taken me with him to walk the creek bed, exploring. We go farther up it, it seems to me, than I would ever go later, on my own, as a boy. The creek here is quiet and overhung and dim. There are only the sounds of wet gravel under our feet, the occasional shifting and clocking of larger rocks, the burble of water. A strange, broken sunlight falls on us through the canopy overhead, and I am following close upon my father, and we are in that corridor of light and water and pre-time together. And while many a soupy, soft-focus depiction of the afterlife may well have influenced this memory, inseparable from my recollection of its details is a very strong feeling, rising perhaps to the level of knowledge, that we are in a place, my father and I, to which we will never return. In fact, even now I fear that I will not be able to revisit us there this clearly ever again, that in committing to words so delicate, so tenuous a memory, I will have made an irreparable trade, and closed the door on the memory itself forever.

Be that as it may. There are so many doors.

When we return home, my father is occupied with several rocks he collected on the walk. He is squatted on the back patio (in the spot where one day Lady would lie down with parvo to die), and he is running hose-water over the rocks before setting them with care in a plastic yellow bucket. In between he shows each to my mother and me, and there is an unfamiliar quality in his voice, something like a note of urgency: the rocks look deliberately shaped. The three of us study them as he turns them over, one at a time, in the wide, wet palm of his hand. One ivory-colored piece, in particular, looks undeniably like a sheep: there are front and back legs, a docked tail, a head with ears. When my father has washed this one clean, he lets me hold it, but mostly what I feel is him beside me, presiding, anxious that I am careful with it. This piece he would set on display in the curio cabinet just off our kitchen, where for the next few years I would often peer in on it, lying flat on its side behind the glass, amid the rows of arrowheads, broken pottery pieces, and a collection of smoothed, oblong rocks we always said were the ceremonial stones of pre-Mississippi's Indians, though on the basis of whose expert opinion I do not know.

ZEKE AND I stepped out on a ten-foot bluff overlooking the creek, holding the dead possum upside-down by the tail and a hammer and nails. Before us the ancient white footbridge of a fallen oak sloped long and true into the cane thicket across the water.

Zeke led us out midway, where the water gurgled loudest in the rocks beneath, and here we knelt. We laid the possum on the wood between us. We turned it over on its back and spread its front legs. Then we each took a tenpenny nail and drove it through one of the little padded possum hands, deep into the wood. We sat back and looked at the weary possum, pinned there against the cool white barrel of the tree.

I said, "Let us pray."

We closed our eyes.

I said, "God, this is Your possum."

I pictured it lying there, nailed-down, weary.

I said, "We are returning it to You now with grateful hearts. And we hope You will accept this our humble offering. But we understand if You don't, because we don't deserve it."

I paused, Presbyterian, to feel how we didn't deserve it . . . then leapt to what I had come to say:

"God, all creation is the work of Your hands and reflects Your glory. Everything is beautiful, and everything is miraculous, and we are out in the middle of it, and it feels like we will never die."

This is what I had come to say, this is what I felt, and having said it I could feel my throat closing, feel the tears coming that would not come earlier, when I had been alone with the possum in the clearing of the vacant lot.

I said, "We are overwhelmed with joy."

Tears tickled my cheekbones. I would not wipe them.

I said, "It is all more than we can say or comprehend."

And reaching for something that would say what still needed, I felt, to be said, I found God's own word:

"You have told us, 'Eye has not seen, nor ear heard, nor has it entered into the heart of man what things God has prepared for those who love Him.' We love You. We believe You. Help our unbelief. Amen."

SLOWLY, I opened my eyes, took in the tear-bleary trees, the bluff, the water—and Zeke.

His eyes had been open a while, you could tell. He was also grinning.

I knew John Dixon sometimes grinned because he was Catholic and so was amazed that people could make up prayers out of their own heads. But Zeke was Baptist. They made everything up out of their heads.

I said, "What."

Zeke tucked his chin, kept grinning.

"What," I said.

We were still on our knees, over the nailed-down possum.

"Nothing," he said finally, and had started getting up, when my eye drifted over his shoulder.

At the end of the tree bridge, on the open sand before the cane thicket, stood Cletus. Relaxed, hands behind, wearing his rumpled middle-aged-man clothes and on his fair, stubbled face what anyone, I believe, would call a kindly smile. The embodiment of a dreamer. When he saw that I'd seen him, he raised his hand in a way that made me think he was going to wave. Instead, he brought an upright forefinger to his lips. Then stepped without a sound, out of sight, into the cane.

Zeke said, "What."

He stood looking into the cane thicket, no longer grinning.

He turned back to me.

"What," he said.

I sometimes wish, of course, I'd answered him differently. But then usually I decide it wouldn't have mattered. Or, as likely, would have made things worse.

"Nothing," I said.

We walked up out of the ravine with our feet crunching in the dead leaves and a cold wind dropping out of a low, sunless sky. More than once I turned, to scan the hillsides through the naked trees. In the street we came upon Tucker Willingham, my three-years-older next-door neighbor, who seemed even more reserved than usual. Sad, I might have said, had I given it more thought. Perhaps he'd been drifting this direction of late. But he was not one to share his mind, and I had long ago grown used to this, and now told myself I no longer cared. At the moment I was also occupied with something I had promised myself to tell him the very next time we met, no more kicking the can. So I told Zeke I'd be up to his house shortly, to see about Wendy, and he left us there, Tucker and me, at the foot of the big hill at the back of the neighborhood. Snow was falling.

# Tucker

SOON AFTER we moved into the neighborhood, my father built me a sandbox. Sounds storybook, I know, but it's true, and I loved that sandbox. My father, I am certain, relished every effort he took to provide it—buying the lumber, framing it out, shoveling in a pickup-load of clean sand—and when he was finished I planted myself in that silky cool bed and played, alone, for hours and days on end. This sandbox sat just inside a gate in the tall wooden fence that surrounded our back yard, also my father's handiwork. And one afternoon, I looked up from my world in the sand to find someone standing in the open gate, watching me.

It was a child. Brown-eyed, summer-tanned, face framed to the jawline in a shapeless helmet of jet hair. That it might be a girl did not bother me. But afterward my mother told me: this was Tucker Willingham, my three-years-older next-door neighbor, a boy. I could not have been more than five years old that afternoon, but I can still see him standing in that open gate, the way he regarded me in my sandbox, the mixture of amusement and haughtiness on his face, the unspoken thought in his eye, the handsome grin. Never has anyone been able to communicate more clearly—and yet so casually our companionship often resembled real friendship—that his happiness in no important way depended on mine. I could accompany him if I wanted, he was fine having me along, or I could find something else to do, it didn't matter to him. And the index of his power in this, of course, lay in its never, in all our years together, having to be spoken. He simply exuded it, as he did cool, as he did confidence. So, naturally, he would always be the boy I would chase: in my choice of bicycle and baseball glove, in my taste in T-shirts and tennis shoes, in the way—when in time he began to groom himself with adolescent particularity—I asked to have my hair cut. I was by no means peculiar in this. Sooner or later most every boy in the neighborhood, I suspect, sacrificed something at this one's altar. But whatever he may have been for them, I can say Tucker

Willingham was for me the first person, other than my father, I ever wanted to be.

He might have taken greater advantage of it. Even so, there were uncommendable moments. He once invited me over to spend the night, for instance, without mentioning he had also invited a school friend of his named Arthur Banger—a loud, freckly, gap-toothed imp with whom I was obviously discussed in advance. The two of them met me at the door that evening, grinning. As well as being loud, freckly, and gap-toothed, Arthur Banger was a laugher. Around him, I discovered, Tucker was an ardent laugher too. And for more and bigger laughs on this occasion they kept waking me up in the middle of the night and telling me it was morning. Their effort to convince me consisted in getting themselves fully dressed (shoes, jackets), setting all the clocks in the house forward ("See, look at that clock over there! And that one!"), then escorting a roused me downstairs to the Willinghams' kitchen table, where they made a show of pouring me a bowl of cereal under very bright lights. Again and again they woke me and, tugging, sniggering, hauled me back downstairs, to that blindingly well-lit bowl of cereal.

I will admit I was confused. Though hardly about the time: the kitchen windows shone black, every unstaged room sat dark, and the entire house, within and without, lay blanketed in stillness, dozing. No, what confused me was meeting so rudely—and repeatedly!—with Arthur and Tucker's apparent notion of me, as reflected in this sloppy, unfunny prank. Did they really suppose that on rising each morning I expected such assistance with my spatiotemporal orientation? That I should find it perfectly normal to be served my breakfast by two people who then withdrew five paces to stand watching me, tittering like lunatics? In short, I did not recognize the person they were laughing at. And when at last, thank you, Lord, the real morning came, I holed up in the Willinghams' upstairs bathroom, feigning constipation, until Arthur Banger went home.

Let me also clarify that I never actually asked to have my hair cut like Tucker's. What I asked was to go to the same barbershop. This I did sometime after noticing his bare ears and missing sideburns, a style he called (I had asked) "preppy." The barbershop was *Frank's*, a little storefront operation where a squat and somewhat droopy-faced man named Frank spent the day in his barber's chair, watching television, while his taller, slimmer, regular-faced partner Lisa used her chair to seat people so she could cut their hair. On that first trip to *Frank's* I took my seat indifferent to the television, the better to watch what Lisa did to Tucker, and when she had done it and Tucker had stepped down looking thoroughly satisfied at what he saw in the mirror, I got up and walked over to where Lisa stood smiling, holding her nylon cape open for me. Having fastened the cape at my neck, she turned her chair around so we could look at me in the long mirror that ran along the back wall of the shop. In a kind, close voice she asked how I'd like my hair cut. I said, "Like it is." Meaning, if I had to say, in the same bulb-of-garlic style it was already in, only shorter. But Lisa misheard me. "Like *his*?" she said. And a thrill went through me. I would never have been so bold as to ask for it. Yet here it was, unbidden, a whole new life reaching out to receive me. A life with a head like Tucker's. I said, "Yes, ma'am."

Lisa was an unobtrusive woman who, in the years that followed, often cut my hair with a wry smile at the idle barbershop chatter around us. On this occasion, however, there were but four of us in the shop, no one chattered, and Lisa's smile, I believe, concerned what she was doing to my head. From across the room Tucker, too, smiled. Goofy with joy, I did what I could to reciprocate without moving my head. And when after about fifteen minutes of all this dizzy felicity Lisa finally pocketed her scissors, put away the electric clippers, and with a comb from her apron laid a scalp-deep, off-center part in the top of my head, she turned me around to see myself in the mirror. I had Tucker's haircut. I liked it very much. Frank swiveled his chair around to join us in looking at me in the mirror. "Well," he said, "it's a free country," then heaved himself to his feet and got Tucker and me some bubble gum. When my mother pulled up to the curb out front, I put my head in the open car door, and she gasped. I said, "Look at my haircut." She did. Then she took me against her side and held me there. Oh, goodness, she said, I looked so handsome, and on the ride home rubbed my back and squeezed my hand, like I'd been injured.

But standing in the open gate of our backyard fence on the day I first laid eyes on him, Tucker's hair still encased his ears, his sideburns hung like turkey beards.

"Hey," he said.

"Hey."

He was, even at that age, smiling that haughty smile of his.

"What're you doing?" he said.

I looked down at the sand, plastic shovel, truck.

I said, "Playing."

He smiled more fully at that, at me, and left.

Even then, I believe, it felt like the beginning of something. I stood up, brushed impossibly at all the sand on my legs and hands, stepped out of the sandbox, and went inside the house. You'll think I am exaggerating, but I do not remember ever playing in that sandbox again.


MY MOTHER was on gracious terms with all our neighbors, but I would not say she was particularly close to

Zeke's mother or John Dixon's or the mothers of any other boys in the neighborhood I considered my peers. Those women never failed to wave whenever they drove past and saw my mother out watering her fern beds. They chatted at length with her in the bleachers of summer baseball games and enjoyed brief visits in the aisles of the Jitney Jungle. But they did not, say, bring flowers around on her birthday, vent to her over sorry relations, or call to report having mishandled the pressure cooker and blown butter beans all over the kitchen ceiling. The woman who did that sort of thing, whose unannounced tap at our storm door never begged explanation, whom I assumed to be on the other end of the line whenever my mother's telephone conversation sounded purposeless, who maintained with her a continuous and unstinting exchange of kitchen staples, pantyhose, jewelry, furniture, holiday decorations, sewing patterns, and those sickeningly ammoniacal home-permanent applications—the woman, that is, who was to my mother as a sister—was Tucker's mother.

Ten years my mother's senior, Miss Sissy kept a trim figure, a smoker's laugh, and the royal, premature opalescence of her hair. She and my mother visited most every day, much of that time while my mother moved about the kitchen and Miss Sissy sat on a swivel stool at our serving counter. Often as not, I would come in from school in the afternoon to find her perched there, arms folded on the Formica countertop before a lipsticked coffee cup, and after standing to hug me, she would sit back down and slap the counter—"Oh, honey, let me *tell* you . . ." —and proceed to tell us something hilarious about Duchess, her grizzled black Chihuahua who fainted a lot, or her easily confused husband Mr. Eddie, or even, in a vein of tender condescension I could not begin to fathom, something about Tucker.

In this way I learned things about Tucker he never mentioned. Indeed, this was the only way I learned anything about Tucker that did not take place in my immediate presence. He simply did not talk about what went on when he was elsewhere, or what, in those long, distant silences, occupied his mind. So from Miss Sissy I heard about a Tucker I did not know, one with middling grades and a quarrelsome girlfriend, a boy who longed for a varsity letter and a pair of expensive white bucks, who got so cold he cried on a duck hunt with his hardier cousins in the Delta, who in the throes of something that defied my imagination punched a hole in the sheetrock wall of his bedroom, then covered it up with a poster (had to be the Walter Payton in mid-flight) to hide it from Mr. Eddie. I listened to Miss Sissy slap the countertop and tell these things, watched her eyes widen and roll, her penciled brows play beneath the stark white hair, her earrings atremble with the open merriment or sham outrage, "Honey, I tell you *what* . . ."—and stood transfixed by the mystery that was Tucker.

OUR HOUSE sat on a corner lot, facing the street that led to Zeke's and John Dixon's, and the Willinghams' sat behind, facing the other. The Willinghams' was a roomy two-story in khaki vinyl, both ends covered to the gables in ivy, its front walk a brick thread in the monkey grass and sweetgum balls. The inside smelled of cigarette smoke chilled by window units, clean carpet, and Tucker. Upstairs, a creaky hallway connected the bedrooms: Tucker's, small and neat and without toys; Miss Sissy and Mr. Eddie's, flickering in the perpetual light of a muted black-and-white television; and at either end of the hallway, with their doors always open, the terrifying, mausoleum-like bedrooms of Tucker's two grown sisters.

These sisters had moved out years before, but they were still around, and I knew them. There was Kaye, who lived in the Delta and with whose husband Miss Sissy sometimes arranged for Tucker and me to ride out there and pick cotton and get laughed at by the field hands. (Miss Sissy drove out to pick us up one afternoon and said, "Y'all, Elvis died.") And there was Caroline, who I believe was considered wayward. She had a baby son named Ricky and a quiet boyfriend with an orange-red afro, and the three of them would sometimes stop by

Tucker's house, apparently just to sit on the sofa. These sisters were so much older than Tucker that I always thought of them as more distant relatives, maybe aunts, and of Tucker as an only child. Nor did I connect them in any personal way with the menace of their deserted bedrooms. What call for theorizing, after all, beyond the preternatural stillness, the implacable stare of scattered keepsakes, the hair-raising chord of silence, absence, imminence? On overcast days in particular, when their sheers glowed like ghosts in the windows, these rooms magnetized the length of the hallway between them—indeed the entire upstairs of Tucker's house—with what I can only call a skin-prickling charge of horrific possibility.

And one overcast December afternoon when I was maybe ten, Tucker and I were alone in his house, eating cheese from the door of his refrigerator, when I noticed he was sneaking looks at me. In deference to the cheese preferences of my father, my mother could not be induced to buy this delicious extra-sharp cheddar, which I had bemoaned more than once before Tucker, so I figured that had to be what he was thinking about. But suddenly—or at least more abruptly than necessary, it seemed to me—Tucker put the cheese away, closed the refrigerator, looked me square in the face, and said, "There is something upstairs I haven't told you about."

The cheese in my mouth lost all flavor.

"What," I said.

Tucker shook his head.

He said, "I'm not supposed to tell you."

All I wanted in the world was to discontinue this conversation. I swallowed the plug of cheese.

I said, "What, come on, tell me."

Tucker took me upstairs.

We stood in the dim, creaky hallway, before the closed door of one of the deserted, grown-sister bedrooms. I was as frightened as I ever want to be.

Tucker said, "Your Santa Claus stuff is in there."

I looked at the black door, at the bar of gray daylight beneath. My mother and father were not heavily invested in the Santa Claus story. They had, in fact, let it fall away fairly early, in favor of playing up the Christ child. What they were invested in, however, was surprising, yea, astonishing my sister and my brother and me on Christmas morning with undreamt-of indulgences and a general demonstration of abundance wholly unknown through the rest of the year. Each year they somehow managed to convince us that this time we'd be lucky to get a pack of Nabs, maybe some fruit, and when Christmas morning arrived they'd wallop us with a spread to rival the cover of the Service Merchandise catalogue.

Tucker said, "But don't ask me to take you in there, because I can't."

I said, "Okay."

We stood before the door, in the dim hallway.

Tucker said, "How much would you pay me to take you in there?"

I found some cheese in my mouth, swallowed it.

I said, "Six dollars."

He had me wait in the hallway while he went inside. After a moment he called for me to come in.

He showed me a cherry-colored wool sweater. He would not let me touch it. He put it back in a crackly brown department store bag and ushered me from the room.

He closed the door behind us. We stood together again in the dim hallway.

I said, "That was clothes."

He said, "So?"

I said, "So, gyp."

For another six dollars, he agreed to take me in and show me something besides clothes.

It was a watch. The exact kind I had asked for, but been flatly told I would not get. It had calculator buttons on it. Again, he would not let me touch it, and after a brief moment we came back out of the room.

We stood before the closed door. I was satisfied. A watch was not clothes.

He said, "There's a lot more stuff in there. It's under the bed."

He took me in three more times, at six dollars per. I have no recollection of the items.

After the last trip inside, we stood outside the door together.

I said, "I don't think I have any more money."

Tucker said, "That's okay, I can't show you any more anyway."

I said, "Okay."

We stood in the dim hallway.

I said, "How much do I owe you?"

He said, "Thirty dollars."

I said, "Okay."

Downstairs, I said, "My stomach hurts. I think I'm going home."

I walked back around to my house with my head full of thoughts.

I walked in through the carport door, into the kitchen. My mother was at the stove, fixing supper.

She said, "Hey, darling."

I said, "Hey."

She said, "Did you find your Christmas stuff?"

"No, ma'am," I said, and stepped into the little bathroom off our dining area and closed the door. This was a half-bath, with walls of cool blue tile and a lavatory and toilet of cool blue porcelain. On the back of the toilet sat a vase of dried flowers and a small painting my mother had done of a chunky little naked girl in a bonnet using a chamber pot. I stood blinking at all this. Then I closed the lid on the toilet, stepped up on it, and leaned over to study my face in the lavatory mirror.

I came out of the bathroom, went to the serving counter, climbed up and sat on Miss Sissy's stool. The other side of the counter was our stove. I watched my mother run a sponge over its already clean chrome surface, among the simmering pots.

I slapped the counter.

I said, "Remember that time me and Tucker went to the Halloween Carnival at Christ United Methodist and we went in the haunted house with Miss Sissy and when she brought me home she said, 'Honey, those boys like to tore my *clothes* off!'?"

My mother took the lid off a pot, stirred it slowly.

She said, "I do."

I laughed.

I said, "That was so funny."

She said, "Yes, it was."

She kept stirring.

I sighed.

I said, "I think so many people miss the real meaning of Christmas."

She agreed that was true.

I folded my arms on the counter, laid my cheek on them.

I said, "Family is just so important."

She agreed it was.

After we were silent awhile I slid from Miss Sissy's stool and headed downstairs to the den, where I could hear my sister and brother. If I was ten, she was five, he three. A brown corduroy sofa sat beside the doorway to our parents' bedroom, and from it I watched these precious children chase each other around the room in witless innocence. I was still doing this when I heard my father come in the carport door from work. The stair from the den to the kitchen was short, and I could hear everything, heard my father close the door behind him, heard him greet and kiss my mother at the stove, put his wallet and keys on the buffet, start down the stairs.

He moved around the den to kiss each of us atop the head, then sat down on our other sofa, an uncomfortable, flower-print job, where he crossed his legs, draped his long arms along the backrest. He had not even visited his bedroom.

"So," he said, "who knows what they're getting for Christmas?"

My brother and sister exploded, leaping, gibbering.

I inspected the fine work done by the upholsterer of our corduroy sofa. When such restraint began to feel conspicuous, I bounced up and threw my hand in the air:

"I know what I want!"

From the calm center of all the commotion, my father looked only at me.

"I didn't ask who knows what they want," he said. "I asked who knows what they're getting."

"Oh. Yeah. Shoot," I said, and turned to leave the field to the jostling innocents.

But it would not have been like my father to let everyone off that easy. And when I dared look at him again, his eyes were still on me.

"How about you?" he said. "Do you know?"

It has occurred to me, of course, to fault him for insisting. I was the one with the burning question here. (I have it to this day.) But as I say, I believe the man was prepared that none of us would get off easy.

And sitting there, looking at me, he waited.

Whenever I come across the word *lugubrious*, I think of that Christmas. Particularly of my father. Of the way he looked at me from our flower-print sofa that afternoon, of the slow, somber way he nodded, mostly to himself, when I had answered, softly, "No, sir." But how to describe the release, the gratitude I felt when, the following day, under the big pecan tree outside the gate in our backyard fence, Tucker did not insist on cash, but with a magnanimity reflecting the spirit of the season, watched me unfold the tissue in my palm, and with that slight smile of his, lifted from it the little ivory piece from our curio cabinet. I was relieved to see it still looked undeniably like a sheep, with front and back legs, a docked tail, a head with ears.

THERE CAME A SUMMER Tucker's pecs were bouncing. He noticed too and rarely wore a shirt. He and a school friend named Teddy Chopley, we learned, had begun a stringent program of lifting weights. Bench press had worked miracles. Teddy came over to Tucker's house a lot that summer, for the two of them to stroll through the neighborhood in flip-flops and gym shorts. Wherever they happened to find the rest of us, they stopped to chat. We watched their pecs. Tucker's definitely bounced more than Teddy's, and you could see the squares in his stomach better too. They declined to join our wiffle ball games, but deigned to loiter at the periphery like sated jungle cats, contentedly massaging and stretching their sore arms, their exhausted legs, offering convalescent chuckles when something was funny, too depleted to laugh. They did also find innumerable reasons and untapped strength to trot short distances in our presence, sudden errands to fetch a sip from the hose, a pine cone from the grass. Just enough of a jog to bounce the pecs.

I suppose they decided this was stingy of them. For out they came one afternoon in socks and shoes to run wind sprints in the street. From a starting line at Sam McBride's mailbox they took turns (Teddy's suggestion) stepping to the mark and blasting off down the pavement—streaking past Harlan Grubb's driveway, past Tucker's driveway—to the finish line of my mailbox, outside the gate of our backyard fence. There, amid the squashed green pecans that littered the pavement, the rest of us stood ready with our digital watches: *On your mark! . . . Get set! . . . GO!*

I can still see Tucker coming toward us, a solitary figure in a sun-splashed street, the shape of him chugging up out of the distance, bigger and clearer with every stride, the muscles in his thighs now leaping and flashing and sliding about like those in a racehorse, his bosom jouncing up and down like a thing tied on with twine. Time and again he blew through the finish line of my mailbox with all our boyhood yearning focused on him, the very and visible limit of what we could imagine ourselves to be. On top of everything else—the muscles, the haircut, the handsome grin—he was faster than we'd have dared to guess. And I believe we would have gone on screaming his times in one another's faces till called for supper, had his exhaustion not dulled the charms of our amazement. On his last run he coasted to a stop beyond the finish line, hocked and spit, turned and presented himself to us with his hands on his hips. "That's starting to hurt my pecs," he said.

THE ONE BOY in our neighborhood not under Tucker's spell was Bo Babcock. This should not have been hard to predict: Bo who was Tucker's age, but a head taller, with a ruddy face, blue eyes, and tawny hair that feathered onto his shoulders, Bo who wore a buck knife in a leather snap-sheath on his belt and a blue-jean jacket in every weather (pushed up the cuffs when he played sports), Bo who stalked life-size animal targets with a compound bow through the trees and bushes in his backyard, assisted his father in endlessly improving their property, spoke respectfully to all adults, was without studied mannerisms, laughed freely, took a visible joy in just being here.

Bo's house and mine were separated by the vacant lot, which more than once he crossed to help me with my yard chores. One Saturday morning, for example, when in the far corner of our front yard, near the street, I was sniveling back and forth along the edge of our neglected rock garden, utterly debilitated before the day-long task of removing all the giant, spiny yellow yucca plants from among all the giant, spiny green ones and hauling them all the way across the yard, the driveway, and the rest of the yard to dump them at the back of the vacant lot,

Bo turned up with a hemp rope, a whetted hatchet, and a jambox full of fresh batteries: "Just culling the dead ones?" he said. With his tools and technique, his cheery and unflagging rhythm, we were done by lunchtime. My mother brought us out a plate of ham sandwiches. We ate sitting on the large, chalk-white stones that encircled a tamed and attractive rock garden, serenely contemplating a job well done and the candy-sweet harmonies of .38 Special.

Bo must have been puzzled by our collective reverence for Tucker, assuming he even registered it. Or maybe he registered it acutely and resented it. Maybe he considered Tucker a smug and preppy threat to all that was right and natural, to what was free and fine about living. But I did notice he made overtures. Having joined a group of us in our sports, he would often at some point appeal to Tucker, literally over the rest of our heads, with some genial observation on their shared circumstances, something country and kind, like "I'm bout out of breath. How bout you, Tuck?" I do not, however, remember Tucker ever rising to these invitations. Or anyone else ever calling him Tuck.

Finally, they fought. The three of us—Tucker, Bo Babcock, and I—were shooting basketball in my driveway, which Bo was not very good at. He stood flat-footed and shot the ball from his chest with both hands, the way gear is flung at new recruits in army movies. In fact, given that one shoots from a point beneath the goal, and that Bo's shot traveled upward in a straight line, without arc, it may have been an actual mathematical impossibility for the ball to go in. Which would explain a lot. But I don't think Bo cared much at all about being good at this game. I believe he just liked to come out and join his neighbors in whatever they were applying themselves to, be it rock garden or basketball.

I do not know what precipitated the fight. Likely a missed shot or two by Tucker, who was of course an excellent player, and some chesty guarding by Bo, who was vigorous. Whatever it was, Tucker stopped dribbling, reared back with the ball, and slammed it off the side of Bo's head. In a blink they were locked together, grappling and slapping. It looked like the object was to climb onto the other guy's shoulders. But then somehow Bo's blue-jean jacket got pulled up and over his eyes, and with this momentary advantage, Tucker put him in a headlock. A headlock, however, that was clearly not going to last. As a matter of fact, because Bo Babcock was taller and happier and country, it was obvious that if this contest continued much longer he would roundly prevail. Which I'm thinking Tucker realized. Because with Bo's head locked precariously under his arm, Tucker hocked the bubblegum juice that was frothing in his mouth, took aim, and spit it, hard, into Bo's hair.

Tucker then turned loose of Bo, backed away to straighten his shirt, and without another glance at either of us, set out across my yard in the direction of his house.

In my driveway Bo stood bent at the waist, in the stance of one who is vomiting and would keep it off his shoes. He struggled not to touch his head.

"Aw, man," he said.

His chief difficulty seemed imagining such a thing.

I turned to watch Tucker reach the far edge of our yard, where he then rounded the corner of the fence, out of sight, without having once looked back.

I went over and picked up my basketball from the grass.

Bo Babcock said, "Michael, brother, y'all got a paper tile I could borrow?"

But by then I was in the carport, on my way inside, and pretended not to hear.

ANOTHER MEMORY of Miss Sissy:

The phone rang, the one on the counter next to Miss Sissy's stool, only she was not sitting on her stool, she was on the other end of the phone.

She said, "Michael, honey, what's your mama doing?"

I said using the bathroom. But just number one, sounded like, if she wanted to wait.

Miss Sissy said, "Have y'all looked in the backyard?"

I said, "Ever?"

Miss Sissy said, "Look in the backyard, quick. Tell your mama."

I said, "Mama!"

From the little blue bathroom my mother said, "Just a minute."

Miss Sissy said, "Y'all hurry!"

I said, "*Mama!*"

My mother said, "*Just a minute.*"

Miss Sissy said, "Y'all looking yet?"

I hollered, "*MAMA!!*"

She came out drying her hands on the lavatory towel. The commode was still running hard.

"What on earth?" she said, and zipped her pants.

I said, "Missy Sissy said look in the backyard."

My mother went to the window at the kitchen sink. Brought the towel to her heart.

I said, "She's looking."

Miss Sissy said, "You too, ding-a-ling!"

My mother said, "Michael, come here, hurry."

I put the phone down, hauled Miss Sissy's stool to the sink, climbed up, and looked out at our backyard.

It was yellow. Bright yellow. The color of tennis balls rolled fresh out of the can. And from one end of our backyard to the other this yellow was flickering and flashing because it was birds: hundreds of them, maybe thousands, flitting, swooping, lighting, but mostly just twitching like little claymation figures all over the grass, the clothesline, the fence, the fig trees, the holly bushes, the swing set, the persimmon up by the garbage cans. Goldfinches, I would learn. In the coming years they migrated without fail, in their season, right through our backyard. But they could never be as many and as yellow as they were that first time, when I knelt at the kitchen sink on Miss Sissy's stool with my mother's hands on my shoulders and the towel from the little blue bathroom damp on my neck.

And Miss Sissy? Out the window, high above our fence, in the curtains of her bedroom window, she stood looking down on our backyard, with the telephone receiver flat on her shoulder. She was smiling, though not like she did when something was funny.

I ALSO HAPPENED to be at the kitchen sink with my mother the afternoon my father pulled his head out of the curio cabinet and said, "Linda, where's that little rock looks like a sheep?"

My mother said she hadn't touched it.

He caught me before I could get to the stairs.

"Have you seen it?" he said.

I said, "No, sir."

He didn't stop looking at me.

I said, "Well, wait."

At the sink my mother turned off the water.

My father said, "Yes or no."

My mother said, "Don."

My father let a long breath out his nose.

He said, "Just tell me."

My mother said, "You're not in trouble, honey. He just wants to know where it is."

I looked at him.

He said, "Just tell me."

I said, "You mean right this minute?"

He said, "I mean this doggone second."

I said, "No, you mean where is it this minute?"

His face grew still as a photograph.

He said, "Yes, son."

I said, "I don't know."

He looked away, came back looking frighteningly patient.

He said, "But you've seen it. Out of this cabinet."

I nodded.

He said, "Okay. Where was that?"

I said, "It's kind of hard to remember."

He said, "Give it a whirl."

I looked at my mother. She was folding the dish towel very, very neatly.

I said, "I believe it was outside. Down by the gate."

In the way my mother was listening without looking,

I could see her support for me whatever the circumstances, her unconditional tenderness. It gave me courage.

I said, "Out by the mailbox."

And letting go of something I could barely believe I was letting go of, I looked my father in the face.

I said, "Trish and Ben had it down there, playing with it."

I then happened to be in the den when my father came down the stairs leading a wide-eyed Trish and Ben. They all went into my mother and father's bedroom, and my father shut the door.

It was a thin door.

From a whole step away I could hear my father begin by asking whether they'd been messing with his shelf in the curio cabinet. But then my mother came down the stairs, evidently just to see what I was doing. This happened so quickly I was not doing anything.

She said, "What're you doing?"

I said, "Playing."

She sent me to empty the tiny trash receptacle mounted to the passenger-side kick-panel of her car.

When I returned, the door to the bedroom had opened and my sister and brother were walking out, she with her chin tucked and quivering, him sniffling. They went to the brown corduroy sofa to hang on my mother. I could not tell whether they had been spanked. My father stayed in the bedroom.

The main sound at supper that evening was our forks. It was late fall and the windows over the buffet were dark, augmenting the cheerlessness. Every now and then my mother or father spoke, but the rock from the curio cabinet was not mentioned. I still could not tell whether Trish and Ben had been spanked. When I finished my plate, I said I enjoyed it, rose to take my dishes to the sink, and as I passed my father's chair, he leaned toward me. I stopped. He took his time chewing his bite, took his time to swallow. He brought his napkin from his lap, unfolded it, wiped his mouth. He refolded his napkin, returned it to his lap, smoothed the wrinkles.

He said, "You're pretty sure about seeing that little rock I'm missing?"

I said, "Me?"

He said, "Yes."

I said, "Oh."

Across the table Trish and Ben had stopped eating. They were looking at me. This felt about like you'd expect.

I said, "Yes, sir."

He nodded.

He said, "I don't think I asked you before, but when was that?"

I said, "Christmas."

With his forefinger, my father poked at the ice in his tea glass.

He said, "Christmas."

I said, "Yes, sir."

He said, "Last?"

I said, "Yes, sir."

He dried his finger on the napkin in his lap.

He said, "Now, would that be Christmas-time, or the actual day?"

I said, "A couple of days before. Maybe."

He said, "Going on a year ago, then."

I didn't say anything.

He said, "It just kind of stuck in your mind, I guess."

I nodded.

He made a face that allowed such a thing does happen, then took up his tea glass and drank. I understood I was dismissed.

As I was moving off, Ben whispered, "Was I alive last Christmas, Trish?"

WHEN I TRY to remember Ricky, the little curly-haired boy that belonged to Tucker's wayward sister Caroline, I find myself thinking of her boyfriend, Ricky's father. I don't remember his name, but he was tall, mum, and punctilious about his orange afro. He wore a black-handled pick in it and was vigilant in keeping little Ricky's hands away. I once watched this young man walk the length of Tucker's driveway on his hands. While he was upside-down the hem of his shirt fell to his chest, exposing the waistband of his underwear, the pale, furred dough of his belly, and when he stood back upright he had all sorts of stuff from the ground on the top of his head—leaves, sticks, sweetgum balls. He stood before Tucker and me smiling proudly, with the blood still in his face, and I felt sorry for him, because he had done this to impress us and seemed to have no idea all that stuff was up there in his afro. Mostly what I remember, though, is him sitting slouched on the sofa in Tucker's den with his arm around Tucker's sister, watching Ricky toddle around the room, chuckling to himself whenever Ricky found a dead bug behind the furniture and put it in his mouth.

Why do I feel something akin to shame in not knowing what became of him?

TUCKER HAD a red golden retriever named Major. He was an outside dog, exiled from the realm of Miss Sissy's Duchess to live in the shade of the sweetgum in the Willingham's front yard, whence he bounced up to follow wherever Tucker wandered through the neighborhood. The animal's affection, however, was indiscriminate.

Whatever hand smoothed his crown, whosoever fingers scratched him behind the ears, Major fought to look you in the eye until, resisting to the end, his own closed in a grinny squint.

On the summer afternoon Harlan Grubb got a brand-new bright-red Honda three-wheeler, every boy on the street piled on to ride. They clung to the gun rack over the front fork, straddled the gas tank, bickered over what remained of the black vinyl seat behind Harlan. Tucker assumed the place of privilege, a spacious cargo deck that jutted from the back of the machine. There he sat facing rearward, in conspicuous luxury, his principal concern to keep his dangling feet off the ground. Harlan drove this crowd around in circles at the foot of his driveway, his tires squashed to the point of making ripping sounds on the pavement, Harlan barely able to turn the handle bars. I watched and kept a short distance. Harlan was a couple of years older than Tucker and already driving a Budweiser delivery truck. He was also a fountain of, as it turned out, grossly inaccurate sexual information. Harlan lived just two houses down from me, between Tucker and Sam McBride, but neither he and I nor our families had ever shown interest in furthering the acquaintance. Thus I hesitated to push in and claim a spot on his new three-wheeler. Besides, before I'd left the house my mother had looked out the window at the scene in the street and said, "I don't want you on that three-wheeler."

So when the brand-new bright-red Honda three-wheeler with boys piled all over it eventually lurched away from Harlan Grubb's driveway, headed off down the street, Major and I fell in behind. The way was flat, and Harlan started slow. Major and I hit a comfortable jog and settled in, casting smiley, sidelong looks at each other. With his coat full aglow in the summer sun, he was one of the most beautiful things I had ever seen, and I thought how very lucky we were to be us.

We wound through half the neighborhood like this, Major and I side-by-side, our footfalls in easy rhythm, our eyes on Tucker, who, gripping the outer edges of the cargo deck, taking care to keep his feet clear of the rushing pavement, watched us with that smile of his. Come on! he shouted. Pick up your feet! he shouted. You better pick up yours! I shouted, and wished I'd thought of something funnier. Others kept looking back to see if we were still there.

Harlan began to find higher gears.

Major and I leaned into it. We grew winded now, our glances at one another became quicker, fewer, if no less radiant. And though something about our situation had begun to frighten me, I drew courage from the nearness of Major's panting, the unflagging click of his nails on the pavement, the sight of his smiling black lips flecked with sugar-white foam.

At this new pace we passed John Dixon Montgomery's house, passed the half-acre vegetable garden beside Runt and Randy Miller's house, passed the turnoff to Stevie and Mike Jr. Taylor's house, and came into what was considered the back of the neighborhood. Here the street turned up in a long, hard climb that lead to the Barrys' and beyond, to where the houses would begin to fall farther apart, the yards grow bigger and rougher (more ant beds, fewer fences), until finally, at the top of the hill, the paved road turned to gravel and the developed lots of the neighborhood gave way to the wild woods of Mississippi. Harlan Grubb started his three-wheeler up this hill.

Not a third of the way up, my legs and lungs were on fire. I put my head down and fought it. I watched my numb feet stabbing the pavement, more and more slowly. When I could bear it no longer, when through the veil of my pain I could no longer hear or feel Major at my side, I looked up.

Harlan Grubb's brand-new three-wheeler was pulling away.

Worse, Major was pulling away.

Why does every story about a boy and a dog have to end sadly? This wasn't even my dog.

I did not make it as far as the Barrys' before I fell back and started walking, slower and slower, until I was standing in the street, dripping and dazed. I was thinking of Major, of how he had taken my falling away. His last glance back had been quick and doggy and far too confident in the largeness of life to offer me any sympathy. His happy eye then returned to Tucker, who had at last drawn his feet up onto the cargo deck to fold them safely under his knees. I watched Major follow the three-wheeler all the way up the rest of the hill, with Tucker clapping and calling to him, until they reached the top, and the gravel road, and disappeared.

I turned and started back down the hill, with the faraway churning of the three-wheeler audible behind me, when the breeze was right.

I followed my tingling feet down the middle of the street, back through the neighborhood, back by my house, to the concrete, guardrailed bridge: the center of the neighborhood, a place of rendezvous and assembly, and no one here but me. In the churchy quiet I leaned on a warm metal rail to gaze down on the lazy stretch of creek, listened to the echo of its trickling from the tunnel of the span, to my spit splat on its glass surface, watched the tadpoles cloud to this event and disperse, watched the somnolent crawdads, the dragonflies. I then took the trail down through the trees to the bank. The light fell softly here on the fetid mud, and my shoes sucked at the edges of the water as I made my way among the rocks, through the cane and tangled vines, over the downed trunks and limbs of older trees, around a long, slow bend in the creek. And coming within view of the spot I still consider my favorite—a small gravel beach in the shade of a wide cottonwood—I halted.

On my beach sat a man.

More accurately, he was squatted there, idly snapping twigs, tossing the bits out on the water, watching them riffle away over the brown and white stones. It was a man I recognized, though I had never seen him this close or clearly. I had the distinct sense he knew I was standing there, contemplating him. But he did not look up from his business with the twigs, and this gave me the impression I had not taken him by surprise.

I looked back along the bank, for the bridge. No part of it visible.

I was, however, still in touch with Major's largeness of soul. And hospitality in such circumstances must not be neglected, *for thereby some have entertained angels . . .*

"Hey," I said, having stepped onto the beach.

He looked up, gave a sort of apologetic smile, an abashed wave.

I said, "What're you doing?"

He made a display of taking in our surroundings, then spread his hands, as if to say you're looking at it.

I nodded, wondering whether he might be mute. I wouldn't have said he looked mute, but then I did not know what a real, not-on-TV mute looked like. Meanwhile, he'd stood, tossed the last bits of a stick out on the water, dusted his hands.

He said, "Do you know who I am?"

His voice was a gentle tenor, almost mellifluous. It had the vestige of a twang.

I looked over at the water, glinting over the stones.

I said, "Sort of. Not really."

He gave a soft, meaningful grunt. I went on watching the water run over the stones.

"Cletus," he said.

I looked at him. He said, "Sort of. Not really."

He gestured in the direction of the neighborhood.

"Some of these little wits came up with it."

He made an effort to smile.

I said oh.

He said, "Yeah. Asking a bit much, no doubt, but I probably would've preferred something like, I don't know, say, Michael?"

I looked at him looking at me.

I said right.

He said, "I guess they think it's funny. Maybe kind of spooky. Backwoods, grotesque, what have you."

I said huh. Could be.

"They wouldn't know it, of course, but supposedly it derives from Ancient Greek, Cletus. To call forth, to summon. So, I mean, it's not uninteresting."

I said yeah. Bet they didn't know that.

"Well," he said, and offered a forbearing sigh.

Brightening, then, he again regarded the scene we occupied, the beach we stood upon, the water and woods, the lushness, the quiet, the beauty.

"This is one of my favorite places," he said.

I looked at it with him, for a moment trying to see it not as I saw it, but as he might see it. I couldn't. I could see it only as I saw it.

I said, "Do you think it will always be here?"

He nodded.

He said, "Sort of."

I said, "Sort of you think so, or sort of it will be?"

He eyed me, smiled.

"Kind of heady, ain't you."

Just then a breath of fresh breeze rose, stirring the thick paper leaves of the cottonwood, and from among the leaves came a fairy stream of eiderdown, so many white wisps drifting dreamily over the water, through our little private theater of broken sunlight. We stood there and watched this, neither of us wanting to move or speak, I believe, for fear of breaking the spell. We were still watching it, when back along the bank, toward the bridge, a stick popped, brush rattled, and a pair of familiar voices came carrying along the water:

"Where is it, Trish?"

"Just come on."

"You see him?"

"Not yet."

Why had I told her? Because there had been a time I told her such things, showed her these places, taken her with me to the creek and the woods and even the Angel's Pond, and when we got home I picked the beggar lice from her socks and pants legs because she was afraid of them and cried. But we were older now, and it was not like that anymore, and I regretted having told her. I would not be telling her any more such things.

I said, "I have to go."

Still watching the drifting wisps from the cotton-wood, he nodded.

He said, "I know."

I took a last look at the flecks of down, floating away against the green of the trees.

I said, "Nice talking with you."

Behind me branches rustled, gravel crunched. I turned to face Trish and Ben, who had stepped out on the beach.

They looked around: at the water playing over the stones, at the airborne seeds of the cottonwood, at me, at each other.

I said, "What."

Ben said, "Who were you talking to?"

I said, "Nobody."

Trish said, "Yes, you were."

I looked at her.

I said, "Just myself."

She put a hand on Ben's back.

She said, "Mama said come home, Michael. It's time to eat."

I SAW MAJOR AGAIN that day, by chance, in the long light after supper. The gang had returned to the neighborhood and unpiled from Harlan's three-wheeler into Tucker's yard, and I happened to look down from our upstairs bathroom window to see them gathered beneath the sweetgum, kneeling and squatting and sitting cross-legged amid the gumballs. Some of them were also petting and stroking Major, who lay stretched out on his side, acknowledging the attention with an occasional, listless thump of his tail in the grass. Tucker was dragging a hose over from the house. Everyone else was still.

When I walked up in the yard, one of the youngest boys, the chronically over-animated, dependably artless Sidney Sizemore, shouted to me, "Major ain't—Major ain't—Major ain't getting up! He got too hot! He got *way* too hot!"

Ignoring him (returned to sucking anxiously at his retainer), I walked over and stood beside Tucker. Stooped over Major, he did not acknowledge my arrival, but with an expression I could not read went on running the clear tongue of hose water around in Major's coat, scouring the brown-honey hair back from the pink skin, while Major just lay there, panting, letting him do it. Major's head was flat to the ground, on its side, so that one eye looked up happily, but at no one in particular, like he was thinking about something none of us knew anything about.

He never got up. He died there on the grass that evening, under the sweetgum, surrounded by boys.

WHAT MAKES US THINK we can decide to change our lives? What makes us think we even understand what that means? *To decide*, from the Latin *decidere*, to cut off. Just so, not long before the start of my seventh-grade year (quite possibly the same summer Major died), I decided to change my life.

I was over at Tucker's, for no particular reason I remember. He was showering in the bathroom off the upstairs hallway, getting ready to go somewhere, probably meeting a girl, and I'd stepped into his bedroom to covet his jambox. I did not have a jambox. I longed for this one. It was shiny red and sporty small and when you pressed its sleek, silver eject button there was the tiniest pause before it consented to lower the graceful drawbridge of its cassette-compartment door—like it had taken a moment to consider what you had asked it to do and concluded yes, this was a reasonable request, let it be so. In describing the jambox to my father, however, I had made the mistake of mentioning it also made a faint humming sound even when turned off, which I liked, because it signaled the jambox was never dead, but ever standing by. My father said it signaled the jambox was wasting electricity. So the jambox I would in time receive for Christmas was blocky and black, sprang open like a mantrap when you pressed the eject button, and assumed the silence of outermost, exanimate space when you turned it off. (In fairness, it did have great bass and was dual cassette.) But on this afternoon my wildest hopes were still alive. I crossed the room to Tucker's nightstand, reached out to finger that lovely eject button, and stopped.

On the nightstand, alongside Tucker's pocket change, his Carmex, and a pile of cassette tapes, lay a small, ivory-colored rock that had once looked undeniably like a sheep. Legs snapped away, ears gone, it had a crude eyelet drilled through the head, as for a lanyard.

I picked it up. Held it in my open palm, taking its weight.

In blue ballpoint, a determined hand, someone had lettered it:

BERRY

I rolled it over. Righted it.

INDIAN DINGLE-

The shower had turned off some time ago and now the bathroom door opened and Tucker came creaking down the hallway, into the full light of his big-windowed room. His towel was wrapped around his waist. Water beaded his muscled shoulders. With all ten fingers he tousled his wet hair, looked at me.

"What," he said.

What? Well, okay, I absolutely deserved to feel the way I felt. I was a thief and a liar and a fool. And, okay, even allowing there are just some things one is slow to see, I was embarrassed out of my mind at how long it had taken me to see what I was just this minute seeing, in particular the part about me being a fool. So, okay, I had some thinking to do, to figure out what this was going to mean for me, for who it was I wanted henceforth to be, etc. But one thing it most certainly meant was I would no longer be

Tucker Willingham's disciple, would not admire or attend him another minute, had set foot in his room, his house, his yard for the last got-durn time. That was what.

Tucker waited, looking at me, still working his fingers in his scalp: as open as he could be to hearing whatever I had to say.

"Nothing," I said. "I have to go."

THERE DID NOT SEEM in the days that followed a non-ridiculous way to inform Tucker of my decision. Yet it would not feel like a real decision, evidently, until I did. And the longer it took, I noticed, the more ridiculous it was going to feel.

THUS IT WAS that by the time Zeke Barry and I came upon Tucker in the street that afternoon with the snow falling and the weary possum nailed to the tree-bridge over the creek behind John Dixon's house, I had made up my mind that the very next time I saw Tucker I would tell him what I had to tell him, even if I did not know how I would tell it. And when Zeke had walked on, leaving me standing there at the foot of the hill with Tucker, I began by studying him furtively, for some help, I suppose, some suggestion in how to proceed.

Through the falling snow I saw his eyes were watery, his nose pink-tipped and numb-looking, the way the cold will make you look, like you've been crying. There was, moreover, no hint of haughtiness or amusement in his face. In fact, as I say, it seemed something beyond his usual reserve might be at work in him. But whatever it was, if it was anything, I had long since taken for granted that I would not be privy to it.

"Hey," I said.

"Hey."

He was standing very still, with his hands in his front pockets, as though entranced by the snow that was streaming down around us like a slow-motion rain. At last he left off watching it, took me in.

"What're you doing?" he said.

We looked at the hammer in my hand.

I shrugged.

I said, "Waiting on Wendy Barry."

He nodded, went back to watching the snow.

I said, "She's up at her house. In her room."

He didn't say anything.

I said, "Her door's closed."

I'm not sure he even knew who she was.

I said, "We're Going together."

He nodded again, politely closing the inquiry.

I had studied him, waited, temporized. There would be no help in how to proceed. But I have always seemed to find the nerve to make myself ridiculous.

I said, "Um, Tucker?"

He didn't hear me. Or maybe it wasn't a sound he felt obliged to answer. Instead, he pulled one hand from his pocket, found a rock in the snow at his feet, and smoothly side-armed it, nailing one of the *Slow Children at Play!* signs that had come with our being incorporated into the city limits.

"My mother died," he said. "I guess you heard."

I kept looking at the sign, wondering for a split-second if this was a joke, but I could hear it was not a joke, and my whole body said not to take my eyes off the sign.

"So that's over," he said, "finally."

I was frantically scrutinizing his voice—"Now nobody knows where Daddy is," he was saying—and at the same time trying to remember, to understand, like you do in a dream when some important thing is not the way it's supposed to be, and you can't remember, don't understand, how this happened or where you could've been when it did not happen the right way. I tried to recall any sense of Miss Sissy, or her absence, at our kitchen counter that afternoon, when I had come in from the bus. My unremitting failure was making my face hot.

Tucker said, "He'll be back. He did the same thing when Ricky died."

I could no longer help myself, and looked at him.

I said, barely, "Ricky?"

But Tucker just reached down, found another rock, and again without trying hard nailed the sign.

"Anyway," he said, "there's nobody at the house."

He put his hand back in his pocket. Sniffed.

He said, "I was going to see if you want to come over."

I looked away, through the slacking snow, at the neighborhood gone ethereally white, the whole world of a piece with the sky, but for the black touches of the trees, the dull palette of beige, slate, olive house fronts.

I said, "What would we do?"

"I don't know," Tucker said. He shrugged. "Eat?"

The snow had stopped. We stood in an empty white tract that was usually a street, watching the lone, belated flakes fall. A confused bird glided over the ground and swung away.

I said, "I can't."

He nodded.

I said, "I got to wait on Wendy Barry."

He nodded again, cleared his throat, and I whiffed what I'm pretty sure was Miss Sissy's Wild Turkey cough medicine.

In the near distance, a tiny figure in tall boots was toiling toward us over the empty white tract. John Dixon Montgomery. Tucker eyed him indifferently.

"Well," he said, "I gotta go."

I said me too.

I watched Tucker Willingham walk a short way down what was usually the street, then cut across what was usually the Millers' half-acre vegetable garden, in the direction of his house. He had his hands in his pockets, his face lowered against the cold and the glare of the snow. It is a handsome image, and the last I have of him.

# Snow Ice Cream and Other Lies

I FELL IN wordlessly with John Dixon, headed up the long steep hill to Zeke's house. John Dixon was a year younger than I and small for his age, except for his head. He lived in a pair of knee-high green rubber boots that right now squeaked like tiny mice on the snow.

"Ooo, Lord," he said, "something stinks."

I said, "Probably me."

He said, "Smells like gas."

I said, "Yeah."

He said, "And dead possum."

I said, "Yeah."

He said, "And fart."

I said, "That ain't—"

He said, "What you been doing with that hammer?"

I sighed.

I said, "Nailing stuff, John Dixon."

He said, "What you been nailing?"

Hand-tool badinage was not my mood.

But I couldn't help grinning.

I said, "Nails."

He said, *"Ahh-glll-ahh-glll . . . ."*

John Dixon had adenoids. When he laughed it sounded like somebody getting strangled.

We walked on with his boots squeaking and our breath-smoke rolling out before us on the sharp, thin air. All around us the neighborhood lay quilted in a magical white hush, a scene so strangely clear and still, with as yet no people or dogs out tracking it up. Only the occasional bewildered bird disturbed the stillness.

John Dixon said, "You ain't cold?"

I was, but had not been thinking about it, and certainly did not mean to walk all the way home for a coat.

I said, "Not really."

He said, "You look cold."

I said, "I'm not."

He said, "Right before people freeze to death they feel warm."

I said, "I don't feel warm, I'm just not cold."

He said, "I'd be careful."

I said I would.

He said, "I had a great uncle froze to death."

I said, "Really? How?"

He said, "I don't know. Got too cold, I guess."

I nodded, welcoming the return to silence.

It did not last long.

John Dixon said, "Mama said she ain't taking me out to Forest Park anymore."

He meant fishing. John Dixon's mother didn't fish, but John Dixon was an only child, and his mother would often take him out to the big, stump-cluttered lake at Forest Park and let him fish from the bank while she sat in a lawn chair and painted her toenails. Sometimes I got invited. We would load into his mother's green Buick and ride out there with several cane poles and more than a couple rod-and-reels run out the rear passenger window, a purposely prodigal bundle that whistled mournfully in the wind out along the highway, clattered like quivered arrows on the washed-out gravel road that descended to the lake, ticked through the high weeds that rimmed the packed-dirt landing. Stimulating trips, whatever their yield. I would miss them. I could only imagine how John Dixon would.

I said, "How come she said that?"

He said, "Don't ask me."

I said, "What, she just walked up and said no more Forest Park?"

He said, "She was sitting down."

I said, "What, she just sat down and said no more Forest Park?"

He said, "She had a hook in her foot."

John Dixon liked to sort his tackle box in the Montgomerys' living room floor. His mother liked to walk the house barefoot. More than once I had heard—from the tranquil vantage of a farther room, the carport, the yard—the unhappy confluence of their separate pleasures. She had a way of yelling *John Dixon!* that could never be matched by a woman who was not his mother.

Could she reasonably be expected then to perceive he was a genius? He had demonstrated it to the rest of us routinely, in offhand ways—catching fish when we didn't, recommending what to cast when we did, sitting riveted through the credits and every last outtake of *Bill Dance Outdoors*—but he had established it sensationally and for all time when he restored to us the Angel's Pond.

For years we fished that scummed black pan for the behemoth bass and catfish of our visions. To which end we bore down on it with all the armaments of our tackle boxes, chunked every gaudy three-dollar lure and ten thousand gobs of greening meat out into its deepest reaches, reeled in every cast oh-so slowly, breathlessly attentive, fairly quivering with expectation . . . and caught nothing. Ever. Not one fish. In those years it became a struggle not to conclude that the dark waters of the Angel's Pond were simply empty, that our efforts here were nothing more than a heavy drilling in bait-swapping and knot-tying, were, in a word, a delusion. As it was, our purpose softened. Our snacks grew larger, more elaborate. We ate them sooner, lingered over them longer, afterwards succumbed to extended and frequently coarse distractions—Bic-lighting our gas, urinating on sentient wildlife. Until finally, except for hauling our gear the better part of a mile through the woods and dropping it in the high grass at the pond's edge, most of us abandoned the burdensome pretense of fishing altogether, and gave ourselves over to exploring.

We had lots to work with. A fantastic network of foot trails filled the woods around the Angel's Pond. Some of these led away to unfamiliar spots along the creek, others wound to isolated coves that by some geometrical trick lay unobservable from elsewhere on the pond's perimeter, still others ended in grassy clearings without discernible origin or purpose. At the end of one trail we mounted a petrified stump-step into an old one-room shack, where bees hummed in the vine that spooled through the empty window frames and the dusty plank floor sounded like the floors in a cowboy movie when you walked around on it. In the curtains of a pond-side stand of willows, we found a chained-up aluminum johnboat. In less aqueous terrain, a mule, not tied up and quite possibly just passing through.

But most beguiling of all, within a cedar grove on the open hill overlooking the pond, stood a derelict, achingly silent, white-clapboard house. And how were we to resist? Crept into the side yard, crouched behind a rust-scabbed butane tank, we spun the saddest, scariest history we could for a solitary and decidedly off-looking man of 50 who had come to shelter beneath that roof—someone, it is true, we never imagined we might ever be, and if without mercy evidently not without inspiration had christened Ol' Cletus. Up, then, we sprang and sprinted across the shaggy, dandelioned grass, a race to the nearest window, to tap at the filthy glass as long as we dared before the first of us peeled away screaming in terror, or squealing with laughter, or both—*I saw him! I saw him! He's in there!*—starting us back across the yard, past the butane tank, for the cover of the trees.

John Dixon was the exception. He never went in for our exploring. And often in our tramping through the woods around the pond, we would emerge from the trees or head-high grass onto some long, broad view of the water, and there he would be, across the way, on a far bank—alone, tall-booted, small for his age—fishing. But on the day he made the discovery that changed all this, none of us had even accompanied him to the pond. I happened to meet him in the street, late that afternoon, on his return. The first thing I noticed was that he carried no tackle box, just a 12-foot cane pole held business-like at the thigh (not on the shoulder à la Andy and Opie) and in that same hand, by its bail, a cricket basket. When he had walked up opposite me, he stopped, and swinging it out from behind his shoulder, lowered to the pavement a cumbrous, pond-smelling stringerful of fish. There were too many to count. A dark Picasso of eyes and gills and fins—gaping, grunting, fanning. I looked up at him. He smiled. "Bream," he said.

And so started us fishing the shallows that footed the open hill, under the gaze of the white-clapboard house. Here dragonflies zoomed like little wind-up toys over a vast mat of apple-green scum, a gooey, buoyant, shore-hugging pad that lay like something sprayed with great patience from an aerosol can but was nevertheless pitted, as John Dixon pointed out, with little craters of brown water, none bigger than a dinner plate. In these, using cane poles rigged with a split-shot and cork, we set down our crickets and worms: for the pound-and-a-half bream that had awaited us here for years. And on fishing out all the open water we could reach from the bank, we followed John Dixon hip-deep into the warm, soft-bottomed pond, cutting tactical paths through the bubbled green mat, then used the butt-ends of our cane poles to send away the loosened shapes, each moving off like some slow, way-gathering barge, leaving behind a fresh expanse of open brown water, in which, for an instant, the dirty-golden bellies of yet more surprised bream flashed beneath the surface. On the walk home our nylon stringers cut into our shoulders, our grip-hands cramped, fish got dragged with curses through the leaves and sticks. Cleaning them was worse. We were fine to scale them with tablespoons, to behead them with butcher knives, but even John Dixon had little stomach for running his thumb inside to draw out the guts and bladders. In the event, our mothers refused to freeze any more. Thus the irony of our leaving, in those years, several hundred pounds of uncleaned bream in the carport of the Old Andersons, a retired couple beside the bridge who liked to host fish fries without children.

John Dixon and I reached Zeke's house with John Dixon's boots still going like mice on the snow and our breath still chuffing heavy and white. When we'd crossed the front yard to the porch and knocked on the door, Zeke opened it just enough to peep out, so that John Dixon's snowball slapped mostly the door, but enough of it sprayed Zeke that he leapt out of the house in his sock feet and chased John Dixon out into the snow (even allowing for the boots, John Dixon was bizarrely slow to be so small) and tackled him. Zeke stuffed snow down John Dixon's shirt while John Dixon kicked and laughed.

*"Ahh-glll-ahh-glll-noooo!"*

I stayed on the porch, and watched.

WHEN ZEKE CAME back out with shoes on, I popped him point-blank in the chest with a snowball in an effort to draw the three of us into one of those idyllic winter diversions available to all adorable children in our early grade-school readers. (I might have remembered these were the same books in which the appearance of a single robin signaled the arrival of spring, which was charming and presumably authoritative, but confusing, as we could look out our classroom window in the middle of raw December and see branches loaded to bending with shabby robins.) Zeke looked down at his snow-splattered chest and said, "What was that for?" It didn't feel like an idea that could survive explanation.

So we got busy stock-piling snowballs, just an obvious thing to be done. Fully absorbed then and free of small talk, we ranged over the Barrys' yard and driveway, dropping to our knees in the pristine places to scoop, cup, and pack the powder, rising to set finished munitions, gently as eggs, in assorted containers: every plastic bucket the Barrys owned, the copper coal scuttle they used for kindling, an antique wheelbarrow they sometimes planted flowers in. We worked intently, without marking the time, our hands surrendered manfully to the cold, our temples running with sweat, and no question but that the effort was meaningful, probably important, possibly critical.

I could have thrown myself at it forever.

But Harlan Grubb interrupted, riding up on his no-longer-new red Honda three-wheeler, towing Sam McBride on an upturned trash can lid. Sam was an admirably upbeat child of divorce whose love (and aptitude, sadly) for contact sport extended to wearing his cleats to school with his blue jeans and, in the yards and driveways of our neighborhood, singing *That's the way, uh-huh, uh-huh, I liiike it, uh-huh, uh-huh* whenever he ran pass patterns or went to the free-throw line.

From the seat of the idling three-wheeler Harlan announced they had come for snowballs. Every single one we had was needed right this minute. Harlan's accent was thick, he was in a hurry, and non-obscene exposition was not his gift, but we understood him to say that at this very moment, at the entrance to the neighborhood, Runt and Randy Miller were perfectly positioned and lacking only sufficient ammunition to ambush the open-cab road grader the county had no doubt already dispatched to come in and clear our streets. I had seen this play out once, a couple of years before. Several of us had watched half a dozen older boys spring up out of a roadside ditch and, scurrying to keep alongside the tractor, train on it a fearsome, rolling volley, surprising to all who witnessed for its profound inefficacy, until, that is, the bristleheaded old driver got his cap knocked off, which brought the grader to a shuddering, diesel-fumed halt that scattered us all. Well, not all. Not tenderhearted Will Melancon—dearest boy, how is it I am only now mentioning you?—who advanced to pick up the old man's cap from the snow, and handed it up into the cab.

Zeke and John Dixon and I piled our snowballs on the trash-can lid and the cargo deck off the back of the three-wheeler, while Harlan of course sat watching from the seat and Sam McBride stood to one side singing *Bo-weem-bo-weh, bo-weem-bo-weh, In the jun-gle, the mi-ghty jun-gle, the li-on sleeps to-night* . . . . When we were done, Sam climbed onto the seat behind Harlan, side-hugging a full five-gallon bucket Zeke told him he could keep because it had no handle. Harlan chucked the three-wheeler into gear, told us to make a bunch more because they'd be back, then made a big slow turn across the snow, and rode off the way they'd come.

Zeke and John Dixon and I now resumed our task in the full knowledge of our purpose, an intelligence that did not supply the fire one might expect. In fact, I noticed Zeke and John Dixon were beginning to kneel and rise almost grudgingly from the snow, slogged to and from our emptied containers with none of their former zeal. I tried to carry us, by occasional word and steady example. Yet I, too, was beset by the thought that our efforts, particularly in conjunction with those of others similarly employed, might be getting out of proportion to their end: how many thousands of snowballs could a neighborhood throw at one old man on a road grader? Still, what were we supposed to do, just stop and say, *I think we have enough snowballs?*

Fortunately, John Dixon got a nosebleed. While he went inside for paper towels, Zeke and I found the curb of the street and sat down. A short-model Bronco with chains on the tires had been crawling up the hill, by all appearances the first four-wheel vehicle to try its luck upon the roads, and here it went crunching by. Bo Babcock's daddy sat inside, his face set like that man's with the hay fork in the Grant Wood painting. He had a hand spared from the wheel to keep his CB mic at the ready and did not risk a glance at us, so focused was he on the snowy way before him, so intense the pleasure of the thoroughly prepared man navigating a secretly welcome apocalypse. The Bronco chugged away up the hill, its rich exhaust the loveliest cotton.

I said, "I wish Wendy would come out."

Zeke was sawing his heel into the snow, to find the pavement.

He said, "How you know she hasn't?"

I said, "You seen her?"

He said, "No."

I said, "Well."

He said, "But I been out here with you."

I said, "Not that long."

He said, "Long enough."

I said, "This ain't a dang bushwhack."

He huffed.

He said, "Well, I don't expect she's going to come out here and start helping with snowballs."

I didn't say anything.

I said, "I know that."

I didn't say anything.

I said, "Anyhow, I'm spending my whole afternoon waiting on her."

He was running his shoe back and forth on a black slash of asphalt.

I said, "I could be doing so many other things."

He said, "Like what."

I said, "Shoot, all kinds of stuff."

He said, "Name one."

I said, "I could be pulling ticks off Lady and burning them in a bowl with matches."

He said, "There ain't no ticks when it's cold."

I said, "That was just a example."

But I should have known better. The boy could be insufferably literal.

I said, "Plus, she climbed the fence again and we haven't seen her."

He finished lowering a stretchy spit into the scar he'd made in the snow, then got to his feet.

I said, "Maybe I'll see if she wants to do something. What does she like to do?"

He said, "I have no idea. She's your dog."

I said, "I mean Wendy."

He said, "I have no idea."

I said, "You're her brother."

He said, "Duh."

I said, "And my blood brother. Supposively."

A bit of a dig, maybe, but this had been the case for months and I'd not yet called it in. There was no chance he didn't remember. Huddled on a sandbar in the middle of the creek, he and John Dixon and I (and possibly others, I can't recall) had scored our palms with a pilfered diaper pin, and when this failed to produce results, only Zeke and I proved capable of jabbing an index finger hard enough to draw blood. Having each squeezed up an irrefutable black bead, we'd sat down cross-legged, facing one another, then reached out to smear and hook our punctured fingers, assuming the severe expression of those TV Indians who clapped slashed palms under an eyeball-to-eyeball gaze that, come to think of it, looked less like permanent friendship than inextinguishable rivalry and defiance. As no power on earth could have induced Zeke and me to look one another in the eye at that distance, we stared at our conjoined fingers.

Zeke said, "How long's this going to take?"

John Dixon considered himself to be officiating.

He said, "A hour. *Glll. Glll.*"

I said it wouldn't take nearly that long and Indians didn't think in hours, being as they didn't have clocks or watches.

John Dixon said, "I know. I was kidding."

Zeke gave a big sigh. He then pulled our hands toward him, so that he could rest his elbow on his knee, which I thought was kind of selfish for a would-be blood brother, but I was getting worried he might quit on me, so I let it pass.

John Dixon said, "The Indians had sun dials."

Zeke said, "I'm fixing to get up."

I said, "Wait, our blood has to *knit*."

Zeke said, "How long does that take?"

John Dixon said, "A hour. *Ahh-glll-ahh-glll . . .*"

Zeke said, "I'm getting up."

I confess that all my life people have let me down in this way—reverting to what is sensible, when commitment to something beyond what is sensible is so obviously what is called for. I realize this marks me for a certain type, perhaps not unfairly considered uncooperative, if not downright solipsistic, the sensible being virtually by definition a matter of agreement, of community, a serviceable standard for a more or less functional assemblage of people. All I can say is I have never trusted the alternative presented by those who would roll clean through this life on the worn-smooth wheels of the sensible, who are not ever and anon moved—by the sheer inexplicability of existence, among other considerations I might name—to the overweening act, who are tucked into their covers night after night by a sweet, bone-deep belief in measurement and moderation, in place of the hammer of philosophical exhaustion. Too pat to say moderation in all things strikes me as indefensibly immoderate? Probably so. But I did introduce this as a confession.

In the end, though, what could I do about it? Zeke pulled his finger away from mine, we stood up on the sandbar in the middle of the creek, and I felt no different whatsoever for being another boy's blood brother. Figured, I said to myself, slopping through it like we had.

Nevertheless, properly speaking, Zeke Barry and I were blood brothers. And somewhat to my surprise, as I sat on the curb in the snow with him standing over me, he seemed to acknowledge it, in that he had let my saying so detain him. He pooched his lips, appearing to consider for the first time in his life the sort of things his sister liked to do. He unpooched his lips, suppressed a smile.

"Brushes her teeth a lot," he said.

I winced.

I said, "See? There you go. What else?"

He studied his foot, smoothing a patch of snow.

"She likes Nile Laters . . ."

Possibly helpful. Women had been wooed and won for centuries with candies.

". . . but she's not supposed to eat 'em. Pulls her brackets off."

I said, "Okay, okay—"

He smiled openly now, on the point of snickering.

"Her wire popped off the other day. Got hung in her lip." He gaped, inserted his finger. "Righ' i' heah—"

I threw a hand up, averted my face.

I said, "Come on, now!"

When he was done snickering, I looked back up at him, figuring maybe it had been worth this monkey business because now he owed me. I could see he felt it too. He sighed, shrugged, searched the sky, shook his head, came back:

"She likes her French horn."

Still no good. In Band I had to glance away whenever she puckered for the mouthpiece. I could not watch the straining and purpling, the bulging veins and neck cords, the throat of a swan turned that of Lou Ferrigno.

I said, "How about movies. Does she like movies?"

He said, "I don't know."

I said, "Who doesn't like movies?"

He said, "Then why'd you ask?"

I said, "How about MTV? Or how about—"

He said, "How about you get up off your butt and go ask her yourself."

And walked away.

"Thanks," I called after him, "blood brother."

Honestly, it was a sad thing to me, the way so many of our exchanges seemed to go. I was genuinely fond of the guy.

JOHN DIXON came out of the house with a paper towel twisted into one nostril and a hankering for snow ice cream. Sick people get what they want. Besides, it never snowed that we didn't attempt snow ice cream. So we scanned the scene for what clean snow remained after the savage harvest for snowballs. Not much. Everywhere we looked, the grubby, prosaic world showed through. We had to go around the outside of the Barrys' house skimming from the window sills, the central-air unit, the back bumper of the disused El Camino that didn't fit all the way in their carport. These gleanings we tamped into gold-rimmed coffee cups that Zeke said his mother never used and had saucers to match if we wanted them, after which we ferried out and stirred in the milk, sugar, butter, egg, flour, Crisco, and the real ice cream you have to put in to keep snow ice cream from being too obvious a lie. With filigreed spoons whose handles were very easy to bend back into place after dipping the real ice cream, we ate from our cups.

Moldered leaf bits. Sharp pieces of acorn.

John Dixon looked up at us, with the blacked and draggled paper hanging from his nose. His eyes were wide, his brow high.

"Not bad, huh?" he said.

Zeke said, "Mine's got roly-polies in it," and slung the contents of his cup out on the ground.

I looked down in mine, at the ashen, crunchy pollution in it, the incontrovertible sorriness of it—and suddenly knew what I would do for Wendy Barry.

The gift I would make her.

The sacrifice.

Yes. Of course!

I walked over and set my cup down on the porch beside the milk jug, sugar bowl, butter dish, egg carton, flour bag, Crisco bucket, and box of real ice cream.

I said, "We have to go to the cliff."

John Dixon had pulled his paper towel out to inspect the pointy end. He twisted it back in.

He said, "The clift?"

Zeke said, "Why?"

I said, "We need something."

Zeke said, "What do we need?"

I said, "*Driven snow.*"

They looked at me.

John Dixon said, "It's at the clift?"

Zeke said, "You want to go all the way to the cliff for snow?"

I said, "This snow here is impure."

John Dixon looked in his cup.

He said, "Mine's got bird mess in it."

Zeke snorted.

He said, "I ain't going to the cliff."

I said, "Why not?"

He said, "All the way to the cliff?!"

"I'll go," John Dixon said, and he walked over and set his cup on the porch beside mine.

Zeke watched him do this, then looked at me. Closely.

He said, "What do you need it for?"

I said, "What do I need what for?"

But of course he wouldn't say it.

He said, "This . . . special snow."

His percipience was unmistakable. As was his disgust. Though both, it must be said, turned out to be deeper than I could appreciate.

I said, "For . . . special snow ice cream."

He studied me another moment, snorted again, and turned away toward the house. I looked at John Dixon.

I said, "You ready?"

His brow went high again.

"Probably not. You?"

JOHN DIXON and I wound our way through an eerily quiet human settlement, following what was usually a wide street but was now just a rutted white tract, cairned here and there with abandoned snowmen in various states of dress and degradation. Along the way we passed John Dixon's house, where a cozy gray smoke rose from the chimney, and farther on we passed mine, where once again I regretted we did not have a fireplace, or any longer even the ceramic-grate space heater my father had ripped out of the den wall to build our gun cabinet, it having at least supplied the enchantment of open flame. What I thought about most, though, was how I was going to get this snow back from the cliff. It was going to take a considerable amount to do this right, to make the impression I would make—no tinkling spoons in dainty cups, I wanted to scoop great balls of this stuff into proper bowls—and I was having difficulty with the notion, for example, of carting *driven snow* in a regular old wheelbarrow, least of all the one propped against the side of my house by the gas meter. For the nonce then I proceeded with no answer, other than that Faith and Hope might not be the greatest, but precious few high undertakings had ever succeeded without them.

At what was usually an intersection in front of my house, the ruts in the white tract we'd been following T-ed into others, and here we made a righthand turn, in the direction of the bridge. From the hill above it, we now heard voices. Bright, pleasant, affectionately reciprocal voices. Certainly nobody we could think of. But on nearing the bridge we came within view of the hilltop, and saw it was the Peterson family, out for a sled.

The Petersons were Episcopalians who lived in an above-the-bridge cul-de-sac I'd rarely visited, facts vaguely related in my mind, their being the only Episcopalians

I knew of. Bailey Peterson was a discreet, tow-headed classmate with whom I was not close, but who had been kind enough to bring his *Book of Common Prayer* to school one day so I could see what one looked like. His sister Nicky was a discreet, tow-headed high school girl I knew as a standout clarinetist and solid hand at bake sales. And their mother was an au naturel gray-blonde with thin lips, wire-rimmed glasses, and a look I now think of as attractively bookish. Mr. Peterson was not with them just now at the top of the hill, having, as he did, a job. (Like my father, he was an engineer at the fertilizer plant.) Plus, I have to think his participation in snow sports was somewhat limited by the glaring limp he carried from childhood polio, though this did not keep him from walking with the Boy Scouts in the Christmas parade, whatever the conditions. Which leads me to note (how these things crowd in!) that Mr. Peterson was maybe the only person I knew who seemed genuinely activated by the civic aspect of such events, where turning up without fail, he exhibited the most credible good cheer I'd ever met with. In sum, I was intrigued by the Peterson family, and very much admired them, but would not have said I knew them well.

Mrs. Peterson I knew least of all. Somewhere along the way, though, I'd heard she was Not Right. As for that, all I could attest to personally was that I'd seen her out playing in the snow once before. This happened when I was in the fourth or fifth grade, probably the same winter we fought the road-grader, when one morning the neighborhood woke to the surprise of a sublime white wonderland and a bunch of us, drunk on the news that school had been canceled, turned out to sled the steep hill above the bridge. We were a whooping horde on cardboard, baking pans, and one flipped-over aluminum RC Cola sign, until Bailey, Nicky, and their mother joined us with an actual sled of glossy wood and trim red metal. I'd never seen anyone's mother venture beyond their yard on foot when it snowed, or a store-bought sled for that matter, and it all felt like a wonderful mistake. Mrs. Peterson clomped among us that morning in duck boots and a puffy parka that slightly floated her arms and had a hood she kept pulled up to frame her smiling, bespectacled, pink-and-cream face, and whenever it was her turn she climbed face-down on the store-bought sled, laughing, making faces of pretend fear, then trailed a long, melodious, motherly *OHHHHhhhhhh . . .* as she left us, heading down the hill. I remember thinking: *She looks fine to me. She looks happy.* But then I also remember, toward the end of the morning, having the distinct impression—as Bailey and Nicky and Mrs. Peterson took their leave, trudging away over the snow, with Bailey pulling their sled behind them on a tether and all three of them holding hands—that it was she who was being taken home.

I came in from sledding that day in tears for my frozen feet. My mother set me up before the ceramic-grate space heater (still in our den wall), removed my shoes, stripped my socks, propped my bare, blanched feet on an ottoman, then found a way to apply hot dish-towels without getting her ottoman wet. I stared at the blue and orange flames in the grate and thought about my feet. My mother came back now and then to check on me, and my feet got to where I could think about other things.

I said, "Mama, what's wrong with Mrs. Peterson?"

She said, "Oh, honey," and shook her head in a way meant to express sadness and sympathy. "She's just Not Right."

I waited, but the only sound was the heater's continuous, dry exhalation.

I said, "She's *deranged*?"

My mother said, "Oh, Michael, I don't know about that."

And she didn't. Despite the lore, everyone in a small town does not know everything about everyone else, everyone only imagines everything about everyone else, and the problem with that is they don't do it any better than people in big towns. Truth was, my mother did not know much more about Mrs. Peterson than I did. Like me she rarely visited their cul-de-sac or had any occasion to meet other Episcopalians, and the only times she and Mrs. Peterson would have socialized were at school functions and summer baseball games, neither of which Mrs. Peterson was wont to attend.

I said, "Is she going to be all right?"

It was my mother's turn to look into the grate of the heater, though not like she was considering whether the answer to my question was yes or no, more like she was searching the flames for some truth that might be available between honesty and good judgment. On appearing to find it, she nodded.

She said, "I just don't know."

And now, barely begun on our way to the cliff, John Dixon and I stood at what was usually the foot of the Old Andersons' driveway and watched Mrs. Peterson come slushing over the bridge on the Petersons' store-bought sled. Her thin lips were drawn and she meant business with her grip on the front crosspiece, but the overall impression was a study in stolen delight. She coasted toward us, relaxing her face, emitting small cries of celebration and relief, and slowed to a stop at our feet.

We looked down at her.

With effort, she turned her face up to smile, then rose clumsily from the sled to stand before us, panting contentedly, while the lenses in her glasses glinted and she kept her chin raised like you do to keep your nose from running. Her parka hood had fallen back, and a strand of her gray hair clung to the edge of her mouth. She felt for it, set it behind her ear, and chuckled.

Were we with a deranged woman?

I could not tell. All I could tell was she was happy. But were you truly happy if you were deranged? Or, for that matter, deranged if you were happy? It was a lot to think on, and in her presence.

In a voice that was pitched and musical, if slightly strained, she said: "Hello, boys."

We said, giving the word a try: "Hello."

And whether at us, or at herself, or at sledding and snow and life in general, Mrs. Peterson gave a short, congested laugh—an unobtrusive, common enough sound that, nevertheless, from deep within her puffy parka, presented to my over-tuned ear the very meat in the walls of her body, so that not only her body, but her entire person assumed for me volume and reality, as when you blow down into a jug and hear, rather *feel*, in your own stomach, its unseen inside.

If she said anything else, I did not hear. As mannerly as I could manage I fled her, jogging ahead of John Dixon, out of the rutted street, into the frozen woods.

I'M AT A LOSS to say just what significance, if any, I attached to that encounter with Mrs. Peterson. But this story is taking its shape from the telling, and to illuminate certain developments I must now enlarge upon my recollection of her husband. The tastefully chipper man of the polio limp, photochromic glasses, chevron moustache. Scoutmaster. Episcopalian. Spousal delegate to the town parade, school function, summer baseball game, where always he was painstakingly democratic in his greetings, shaking hands with even the smallest boys and addressing us all as young men, as though each of us were full of promise and he would keep an eye out, eager to see what fine things we would accomplish. In all this, in his patient, attentive way of limping through the world, there was about Mr. Peterson an exotic whiff of optimism. Which by nature I suspected, as I did anything exotic, even while thinking him probably the most appealing adult I knew. We were not merely Presbyterian, but of the unabashedly Calvinist stripe, so I was not raised to believe in good people. But good people, I would have to say, are the most compelling glimpse I've had of Goodness. And whenever in my life I have chanced to meet or so much as recall him, Mr. Peterson has offered to guide.

I have dwelt on the man's good cheer. Equally evident, however, was what I think of as his honesty. There was something in the way he entered a crowd, the way he addressed people, the way he looked at you: he just seemed un-subject to the fear that makes others of us ignore things, like people and their pain. About his manner in this there was an unmistakable hint of choice. Perhaps even of formality. Or, better, form. But certainly nothing prim or prepared or, least of all, rigid. Rather the opposite: he seemed to have achieved in his bearing, by his choice, a sustained demonstration of openness, a continual and un-resented relinquishment. And yet—isn't this true?—it did still seem he was doing a thing he was supposed to do precisely because, whatever his personal inclination, he was supposed to do it. He seemed honest even about that.

I notice these qualities in the man have always seemed corollary, in my mind, to his Episcopalianism. I suppose there is no accounting fully for such circumstantial connections. All I could glean from my theological inquiries of Bailey left me vaguely uneasy at his being somehow both crypto-Catholic and doctrineless. His *Book of Common Prayer* was a perplexing thing, full of remarkable, if at points obscure poetry, arranged in patterns and services I did not recognize (*Collects? Compline? Ministrations?*), enlisting a great deal of language I distrusted as extra-Biblical. But embodied in Mr. Peterson, this unfamiliar, perhaps aesthetically bewitched cousin in the family of Christendom seemed to me so profoundly—in a word—civilized. In him it seemed to answer all the oppressive strangeness and beauty of this life in a gentle and knowing spirit of paradox. In him it seemed to say, Yes, existence is indeed a flipping miracle, and if you care to see aught below the surface you must not swoon or rant or panic, but dial it back a touch, young man, and risk the restraint to settle in, deep enough, long enough, to observe the endless and exquisite ramification—from surface to bottom and back again—and even to glimpse, if you should be thus blessed, the true scope and nature of what is so miraculously on offer: what we, crushed by our wonder and our longing and our inability to summon the Name of Names, have denominated Love.

"WHAT IS THIS, John Dixon?"

We were lying on our backs, looking up through the icy treetops into the gray sky. Our feet were heavy, our thighs ached, our panting had subsided.

He said, "I just need two more minutes."

I said, "No, I mean all *this*."

I held my arms open to the sky, the treetops, the glowing white woods around us.

I said, "How do we even know this really exists?"

John Dixon got to his elbows. His head looked too heavy for him. He squinted around at the woods, at me.

He said, "Do what?"

I said, "Take you, for instance. How do I even know you're real?"

He said, "How do I know *you're* real?"

I said, "It ain't a cut-down, I'm just asking."

He let the weight of his head pull him back down to the snow.

We were silent again.

A gorgeous, haunting wind came moaning through the treetops, set them creaking in their sheaths of ice, tinkling like winter palace chandeliers.

I said, "Can I tell you something, John Dixon?"

I was disappointed he took it rhetorically, but pushed on.

I said, "I think something big and important is going on. I just don't know what it is."

That I might have to carry this conversation seemed fair.

I said, "I don't know what to do about it, either."

The wind continued its moaning, the treetops their creaking, tinkling. I tried to think how else to say it.

John Dixon said, "You think fish hurt when you hook 'em?"

It did not feel like a time to be selfish with our line of inquiry.

I said, "I think it depends."

He said, "Well, like when you set a number four hook and it comes out their eye."

I said, "I mean depends on what you mean by *hurt*."

This had been my father's answer when I'd asked more or less the same question—not unusual, I suspect, among non-psychopathic boys who fish—and it made me feel both very smart and somewhat deceitful now to have such a fine answer ready to hand. I had very much liked what my father went on to say—*Hurt is a people word, not a fish word, so no, probably not the way you mean it*—because it sounded strange enough to be right. It also, not incidentally, eased my concerns on the subject. I just hoped I could say it all as well as my father had.

But I'd taken too long to start.

John Dixon said, "You think we live forever?"

Such were the rigors of his friendship.

I said, "Well, who's we?"

He said, "Everybody. Anybody."

I said, "Those ain't the same."

He said, "Okay, me and you."

I said, "Well, do you mean me how I am, right here, and you how you are, over there?"

He said, "However. Wherever."

I said, "Well, . . . —dang, John Dixon, I don't know. I started out with something to say but this conversation's gotten confusing."

He said, "I wouldn't worry about it. I get confused all the time."

But I wasn't worried about it. In fact, I was already no longer thinking about it, my attention having been arrested by something in my view of the sky: beyond the cloud of my breath had flashed a bolt of pale gold.

I stopped my breath.

Didn't blink.

There! Again! What the—?

I sucked air and sat up.

And the next one hit me square in the chest, bombing me with ice and dirt—a length of dead yellow cane went spinning off across the snow.

I leapt up and took off through the frozen trees, closing on Zeke before he could uproot another spear of cane, and when he broke and ran I chased him down, and when he fell I pelted him with snow, until he quit resisting and just held his hands up to keep it out of his face. I was kind of figuring at some point we might laugh, but we didn't. I helped him up. The two of us started trudging back to John Dixon, still reposed on the snow.

I said, "Thought you weren't coming."

He kept his eyes on the ground.

Was there a trace of a grin?

He said, "Changed my mind."

John Dixon lay with his hands behind his head, as if in peaceful sleep. When he opened one eye, we were standing over him, arms cocked, snowballs double-packed.

He said, "Personally, I think we might live forever."

STUNTED JUNIPER grew thick atop the cliff. We pushed our way through it, fighting to see our feet, branches slapping us in the face, dumping snow down our necks, until of a sudden we were not getting slapped in the face or dumped-on because we stood, three abreast, at the cliff's edge.

A carpet of grizzled treetops ran to the horizon.

Out on the carpet, beyond the Angel's Pond, sat the lusterless white ellipsoid of a water tower. On top of it a small red light slowly died, slowly revived, slowly—whoa! A kiting buzzard planed across our faces.

We got busy throwing stuff off. Pickings were not as slim as they might have been out here on the lip: some fire-ring rocks, a couple of mud-choked bottles, one half-burned car tire. Well after the last had bounded to the bottom and leapt, freakishly high, into the tree line, John Dixon continued to look over the edge.

I said, "What."

He had his chin out, was peering hard down his nose to see what he could see.

He said, "How much would y'all pay me to jump?"

Zeke and I sidled to the edge, looked over.

Zeke said, "Fifty cents."

John Dixon looked at him, huffed, and went back to peering over the edge.

He said, "A dollar."

With my whole heart I wanted John Dixon to jump off the cliff. Who wouldn't? But I had mixed feelings about paying him for it. Zeke remained quiet now too. The three of us were still peering over the edge.

John Dixon said, "Seventy-five cents."

Zeke said, "You won't jump."

John Dixon said, "All right, fifty."

Zeke said, "You won't do it."

John Dixon said, "I will if you pay me."

Zeke said, "I ain't paying you."

John Dixon said, "You said fifty cents."

Zeke said, "I ain't paying you."

John Dixon said, "You said!"

Zeke said, "I ain't even got fifty cents, John Dixon."

John Dixon turned to me: "He said fifty cents!"

Zeke said, "I was just playing, idiot!"

John Dixon looked at him, and ceremoniously shut his mouth.

The breeze soughed in our ears, watered our eyes, bobbed the snow-laden limbs of the junipers.

John Dixon said, "I'm goan tell everybody what you said in your sleep at my house."

Zeke said, "What."

John Dixon said, "About Louise Mandrell."

Zeke's face got splotchy.

He said, "I ain't paying you."

He then turned away, and pointedly began looking for something else to throw off. But I kept an eye on John Dixon. And in the end he did not jump.

It was more like he leaned out and offered his little body to gravity.

Zeke must have seen him too, because we both shouted and met at the point of departure, sticking our necks out as far as we dared, to follow John Dixon's progress. By then John Dixon had already stopped falling free and begun to bang and roll down the long, exposed face of the cliff, tumbling and crackling through the sparse vegetation, sending up sprays of snow, all the while crying out and trying to grab at the collapsing shelves of snow and earth that were sliding along with him, a foaming surf of black and white and him unable to stop or slow or right himself, and in this way arriving at last at the foot of the cliff, where he skidded several yards head-first, on his back, before his green boots shot straight back over his head twice in succession and—*thump*—he slammed against some squat, immovable object in the snow. The squat, immovable object rattled like a padlocked shed door.

Zeke and I stood squinting into the breeze.

John Dixon lay face-down, crumpled, not moving.

Zeke said, "He ain't moving."

I said, "Not yet."

He said, "Move, John Dixon."

I said, "There he goes."

John Dixon rolled over on his back, writhed his legs. Even at that distance we could see his chest convulsing, hear the breathless *oh . . . oh . . . oh . . .*, until the sound died. The writhing and convulsing ceased.

We strained to listen.

". . . *ahh-glll-ahh-glll* . . ."

Zeke wheeled and swatted snow from the trees.

"Idiot!" he said.

I said, "Who?"

He said, "Why didn't you grab him?"

Which didn't exactly answer my question.

I said, "Why didn't *you* grab him?"

He said, "What's he saying?"

We leaned back over the edge.

John Dixon had sat up. He was brushing snow from the object that had sounded like a padlocked shed door.

Zeke and I hollered, "Whaaat?"

John Dixon hollered, "I said 'Hey, I found something!'"

He had cleared the face of it. And getting stiffly to his knees, he began to clear the top. It looked like a small, boxy piece of furniture. A chest maybe. Or . . . a trunk?

*My driven-snow container!*

*See?*

*I knew it!*

John Dixon was on his feet, hobbling around the object, dusting at the remaining snow. He had it almost clean, and I could see it was just as I had thought but could scarcely permit myself to believe: a roomy, barrel-top trunk, with vintage fixtures, reliable-looking handles, and surely no rival in my world for *romantic*.

A lump of humble gratitude came into my throat. *I will lift up mine eyes to the hills—from whence shall my help come?* And how paltry had been my Faith, my Hope.

John Dixon was leaning over the lid, examining something. He straightened and turned to us.

"It's a time capsule!" he hollered.

Zeke and I looked at one another—did he say what we thought he said?—then back over the cliff.

Zeke hollered, "Did you say, a time capsule?"

John Dixon hollered, "Yes!"

Zeke hollered, "Are you sure?"

John Dixon hollered, "Yes!"

I hollered, "How do you know?"

John Dixon hollered, "It says!"

I hollered, "What does it say?"

John Dixon bent back over the lid:

"This is . . . a time . . . capsule!"

IN THE SHADOW of the cliff, we stood before the object in awed silence.

An honest-to-goodness time capsule.

An inscribed brass plate on the lid said so.

Well, this did complicate my humble gratitude.

One of the indisputable success stories of our elementary school curriculum (not one grade, I believe, left the notion untended), time capsules had long obsessed us. How many aluminum-foil-lined shoeboxes had we buried in these wooded hills? On how many cassette tapes had we introduced ourselves to Soviet invaders, extraterrestrial colonizers, survivors of the Great Conflagration? How many deliciously anguished partings had we made with dearest personal possessions—pocket knives, base-ball cards, prized decals we had intended for our dresser mirrors—offered up to render our way of life? But what a blundering oversight, it suddenly seemed, that no one had thought to mention we might one day find ourselves on the receiving end of someone else's attempt to shine a kindly light from another time. For all the thought we'd given that possibility, the specimen before us may as well have come from the future. And taking in this sturdy chest, with its exposed hickory staves and iron catches and the whole thing sitting (a further reproof) in plain sight upon the ground, I for one was profoundly chagrined.

What were our shoeboxes compared with this?

It is a truth worth recording that a boy will not merely endure, but invite genuine suffering as part of what he knows, at some level, to be the pleasure of pretending. Hardship lends the illusion weight, depth, sweetness. Indeed, a pretending for which one has not in some mea-sure suffered is so easily dropped, so *thin*, it feels hardly worth the bother. But mind: let a boy's awareness he is pretending rise too near the surface, let the unvarnished image of him at his play be caught and shown him, say, in a quarter panel's lacquer, or the glass of a patio door—and the pleasure in it dies. The pretending, formerly so free and easy, turns toilsome as sit-ups. And where that pre-tending has been nursed richly on some hardship, some boy-measure of suffering, an extravagant bitterness may set in, an enervating sense of the absurdity of all creative endeavor. Which is perhaps to over-say: though I'd never supposed anyone would actually find our pocket knives, baseball cards, or unspoiled decals, it now wounded me deeply we'd buried them in shoeboxes lined with aluminum foil and called it a time capsule.

And how, on top of this, did I feel about commandeering someone's stirring achievement of the genuine article to haul my snow? Not so good, I can tell you. And even assuming I got okay with that, what were we going to do in the meantime with all the very personal, meaningful stuff inside? Come to that, what were we going to do with all the very personal, meaningful stuff inside even if I didn't get okay with using the trunk to haul my snow? I just had so many questions.

We clubbed the ice off the front hardware, got the catches levered open, and lifted the barreled lid. With this there rose the pleasantly musty odor of a roomy wooden trunk—with nothing in it.

Or almost nothing.

On the floor lay something flat, sleeved in brown paper.

Zeke stood at the other end of the trunk from me, and he reached in and picked up what turned out to be a brown bag, pulled from it what appeared to be a magazine, and looked at the cover. Kept looking at it.

John Dixon, standing between us, stepped over to look at it with him. They were very still.

John Dixon said, softly, "Open it."

Zeke did, and now I could see the cover.

It was a naked-woman magazine.

I looked away, Presbyterian, to think just a second about this. And when I did I saw, on the floor of the trunk, in the spot where the sleeved magazine had been, a piece of white paper. I reached in and picked it up. A folded piece of notepaper. I unfolded it. I read the two sentences written there. Read them again.

I looked at the trunk.

I looked at the woods around us.

Ice had begun dropping from the trees, puffing on the snow.

*. . . sick . . .*

*. . . suffering . . .*

*. . . afflicted . . .*

Once more I read what was written on the paper. Then refolded it, and put it in my pocket.

Precisely because I was Presbyterian, in the properly Calvinist vein, I could admit being not invulnerable to a not-too-trashy naked-woman magazine. And under other circumstances, well, who was to say. But at present my mind was almost painfully crowded. It was hard enough coming back from the awfully serious words I'd just read to the awfully muddled errand I was on, let alone to a passal of nude women. Added to which, I didn't relish the image of me, standing alongside Zeke and John Dixon, looking the catatonic way they did right then.

I said, "Well, I guess we better head back up."

John Dixon looked at me over the magazine. He then looked behind him, at the towering slope of shredded snow and earth and broken brush, and back at me.

He said, "Up on the clift?"

Zeke, whose eyes had not moved from the magazine, said, "Why?"

I said, "I reckon we still need that driven snow."

It was not an easy sentence to mouth. The silence that followed was worse.

I said, "You know, for the ice cream."

Zeke still did not take his eyes from the magazine.

He said, "Is that ice cream for my sister?"

I said, after clearing my throat, "Maybe."

He now looked at me over the magazine.

I said, "I mean, if she wants some I was thinking I could give her a little of mine."

He said, "She can't eat ice cream."

I said, "She can't do what?"

He said, "Yeah, I got to thinking about that after y'all left. About how Wendy can't eat ice cream. Doctor told her not to."

I said, "Bull."

He said, "Bull, I'm serious."

I said, "Bull, who can't eat ice cream?"

He said, "My sister," and grinned.

I said, "What's her problem?"

John Dixon said, "Some people can't eat chocolate."

Zeke shrugged. He said, "When she eats it, she throws up."

John Dixon said, "I throw up near every night."

Zeke said, "She gets foamy ice-cream throw-up all in her braces."

And baring his teeth, he pointed, circling his finger where the foamy ice-cream throw-up would be, all in her braces.

John Dixon said, "*Ahh-glll.*"

Zeke and I stared at one another.

The revelation did kind of simplify things, I admit. The crowding in my mind was already less painful. But he had not meant to do me any favors.

I said, "How come you're just now telling me?"

Zeke went back to the magazine.

He said, "How come you didn't ask me about it?"

This seemed hateful to me. And I might well have pursued it, but for two things. One, I got stuck trying to think how to answer him. Two, I had something else

I needed to think about. Namely, some remarkable words, on a paper in my pocket, from Ol' Cletus.

# Melancon

I WALKED OUT of the woods in the equivocal light of late afternoon, into a neighborhood from which the magic had melted with the snow. By some true measure I had been away decades. Behind me, at the foot of the cliff, I'd left Zeke and John Dixon zombied before the naked-woman magazine, no audience for any explanation. This was expedient, as I could have easily enough said where I was heading, but not so easily why, and I believe having to try might well have deterred me. Indeed might yet. But this I can say: the words in my pocket were alive in me. In the intimate solemnity of their petition I heard something that both asked of and supplied to me courage, breadth of vision, belief. A state in which going where I was going made an undeniable, if as yet hazy kind of sense. I should add that, as a rule, whenever it seems to me the universe is trying to make sense, I like to help it. No surprise, perhaps, being as I am part of the universe. "... *soothe the suffering* ... *pity the afflicted* ..." entreated the paper in my pocket. And so guided, I stepped out of the dripping trees onto the pavement at the bridge, and started up the hill for the Melancons'.

Will Melancon and I had become fast pals in the fourth grade when his family moved into the neighborhood from Louisiana with their swamp-French surname—*Muh-LAWN-sawn*—and a full-size pool table in their basement. They were unfussy people who stocked branded snack foods and welcomed me any time. My only quibble was that, often as not, whenever Will and I climbed the narrow, squeaky basement stair into the window-lit stillness of the Melancons' kitchen, his father would be sitting on a stool at the serving counter, staring at us. This might be in the middle of the day, in the middle of the week. There was never anything on the counter before him but a pack of cigarettes, a lighter, an ash tray, maybe a coffee cup, and he was never doing anything but watching us top the basement stair, except, on occasion, mumbling over his shoulder to Will's cheerful, red-headed mother, swishing around the kitchen behind him in her nurse's uniform. "Well, hey, handsome boys!" she'd cut in. "Whatcha know good?"

When he was not sitting at the serving counter, Mr. Melancon often spent the middle of the day, in the middle of the week, shuffling around the house and yard in his moccasin house shoes and a tucked-in, V-neck undershirt. A small, nimble-looking man, he was nevertheless a slow and neglectful mover, a heel-scuffer, who left his cigarette untended in his lips for long stretches while he did non-urgent things with his hands. To be fair, you would not have said the man was mean, or even rude, but you would never have mistaken him for friendly. And I, no offense intended, did not care to linger in a room with him.

One afternoon Will and I were in the basement shooting eight ball. He was up on his toes, stretched out across the table.

I said, "Does your daddy have a night job?"

*Glance!*

For a guy who owned a pool table, Will was not very good on it. He was, in particular, one to miscue. He came back down to the floor, sighed into his thin brown bangs.

"Nuh-uh," he said. Then, with interest: "Does yours?"

I CAN SEE HIM at it still: short like his dad, he would go up on his toes to stretch out across the table, and there, straining to hold the pose, would bear down on the cue ball with an almost unsightly degree of focus and determination, drawing the powdered blue tip of the cue all the way back, easing the powdered blue tip of the cue all the way forward, drawing it back, easing it forward, drawing it back, and—*glance!*—send the ball wobbling off across the felt in the least desired of directions. It may well be the ugliest sound in sports, certainly one of its most dispiriting sensations, sister to the perfect pitch squibbed off the end of the bat. By comparison there is something well-nigh satisfying about taking aim on a ball and missing it entirely. And yet afterward Will would simply come back down to the floor, shake his head, maybe roll his eyes, and puff that little sigh of his into his bangs.

In fact, though it makes me uncomfortable to say so, Will often seemed to me in some way born to such disappointment. His every mannerism was softened by a modesty that seemed privately cosmic in origin, and in that sigh of his I could hear what sounded like, if not resignation exactly, then a sort of philosophical acknowledgement of all the unseen things he was up against. Whatever it was left the boy with zero instinct for posturing or pretension. A deficiency, needless to say, I did not share. Consequently, I could be startled, as when he once flat-out admitted he wished he were better at basketball and asked if I would help him with it.

That's how we came to spend an afternoon in my drive-way with him dribbling around me in obedient circles and me blowing on a whistle I'd dug out of my sister's toy box. Now and then I shouted for him to switch hands, feinted at the ball, helped him chase it down when it shot off his foot. In the meantime I discovered and remarked for his benefit that *drills* and *skills* rhyme. Because it was muggy out, I also granted straightaway his eventual request for a timeout to remove his shirt. But here a curious thing happened. When Will had tossed his shirt onto the trunk of my mother's car and resumed my assignments, I could not help noticing, in the very middle of his otherwise slight person, a dimpled and jiggly little belly. Dribbling and hustling again, he did not seem the least conscious of it. And it struck me, though I cannot explain or defend it, that what I was watching was a very kind person striving to do difficult things meant for someone else. This was not pleasant. Indeed, it bled a great deal of the pep from my effort, and much sooner than I had intended I gave a last, long blast on the whistle, yelled "Good job!" and suggested we knock off for the day, before dark fell and the bugs came out.

TO MY RELIEF, one lesson appeared to satisfy Will's interest in roundball. We returned to the pool table, to our horns (my cornet, his alto sax), to the sofa in the Melancons' tidy, somewhat spare, not especially homey-feeling living room, where we played Atari or found something on cable. One memorable afternoon we found cinematic Marines in a cinematic Vietnam sneaking through the bush in cinematic half-light. They wore face paint and had grass in their helmets. A firefight was imminent. I pshawed.

I said, "My daddy hates this movie. He says it wasn't nothing like that."

Will's mouth was full of Bugles. He raised his chin to keep from losing any.

He said, "They stand too close together."

I said, "They shoot the M60 way too fast, too."

He said, "I know. Supposed to be three- and four-shot bursts."

I said, "I know. Or you'll overheat the barrel."

He said, "I know."

We took turns in the box of Bugles between us and watched the Marines get into their TV firefight. They lobbed grenades, shot up the lush countryside. Grass and dirt flew. Men screamed.

Will, however, had begun a soft, tuneful humming. I knew the tune. I knew some words for it, too. I'd heard other words sung to it, in movies and TV shows, but they were never the words I knew. Under his breath, Will sang:

"*I want to be an Air-borne Ran-ger . . .*"

I choked down pointy, unchewed Bugles to join, under my breath:

"*I want to live a life of dan-ger . . .*"

Will sang, a little louder:

"*I want to go to Vi-et-nam . . .*"

Together we sang out:

"*I want to kill a Vi-et-cong!*"

We laughed. This was wonderful!

I said, "How'd you know that?"

He said, "My daddy was there."

I said, "Mine too! Who carried the sixty in yours's squad?"

He said, "Janowski at first. But he got shot in the throat. So then it was Abrams."

I said, "Mine's man was Copeland. His third tour. Kept re-upping because he didn't have anybody to go home to. And didn't get one letter, the whole time. I think he just wanted to die over there."

Will nodded solemnly, for poor Copeland.

He said, "Some guys my daddy knew set up a claymore to take out their own lieutenant while he was sleeping, and they set it off, and the guy died, but it was the wrong guy."

I nodded solemnly, for the poor wrong guy.

I said, "One time my daddy and them were on patrol, and this guy McElvoy was carrying a grease gun—"

"Oh, no." Will shook his head. "They're bad about going off on you."

"I know. McElvoy set his down butt-first on a rock and it went off and shot him in the mouth. Bullet went through his teeth, roof of his mouth, behind his nose, and out his eye, like this." I showed him with my finger. "McElvoy just stumbled back and sat down. Face covered in blood and meat, mouth messed up pretty good. But he could still talk. He told Doc, said, 'Just give me a shot. I ain't afraid of dying, but give me a shot so I don't hurt.'"

Will said, "Shoot, I don't blame him."

"Me neither," I said. "But Doc kept telling him he wasn't dying. And son, that made McElvoy mad. He reached out and found Doc with his hands, like this, pulled him in close and said, 'Doc, I just shot myself in the face with a grease gun. I'm dying. Now give me something to keep it from hurting.' But Doc got McElvoy's face wiped off, and McElvoy realized he could still see out of the one eye. So he told Doc to reach over there and get the Polaroid out of his pack and take a picture of him. Which Doc did and handed it to him. McElvoy held it up to his good eye and said, 'Huh,' like maybe he really would make it, then got up and *walked* over to the chopper they'd sent for him. My daddy and them never saw him again."

Will shook his head. "There it is."

I said, "Guy was getting short, too."

Will said, "Mmm."

I said, "Yep."

But I was feeling my story had gone a little long, dropped our momentum. I tried to pick things up again.

I said, "There's no baser form of life than a soldier in a combat zone."

Will nodded.

He said, "There's no smell in the world worse than burning human flesh."

I said, "The night belongs to Charlie."

He said, "I know."

I said, "It might sound fun, lying around in your bunk shooting soap rounds at snakes crawling through the walls of your hooch, but it's really not."

Will said, "Sitting around waiting is the hardest part."

I said, "I know."

Will said, "I'd a lot rather be fighting, getting shot at and shooting back, than sitting around waiting."

I said, "Shoot, I'd rather have VC pouring in over the wire as to be sitting around waiting."

He said, "Shoot, me too."

We lapsed into thoughtful, Bugle-munching silence.

On TV the Marines were on R & R. They raced down a beach in Hawaii in colorful shorts and necklaces of flowers. They ran splashing through the waves with attractive women in bikini swimsuits.

Will said, "Where'd your daddy take R & R?"

I said, "Tupelo. Where'd yours?"

"Mandeville."

"Is that in Hawaii?"

"It's in Louisiana."

I said, "Me and my mama were living with my mamaw and papaw, but my daddy took us to a motel for a week. It had a swimming pool, a high dive, coke machine, *everything.* It was so cool."

He said, "How old were you?"

I said, "Six months."

He said, "I wasn't alive yet for mine's."

I said, "My daddy kept waking up in the motel and reaching for his M16."

Will said, "You just get so used to having it with you."

I said, "I know."

The Marines on TV were kissing the attractive women at night on the beach.

Will said, "Did your daddy kill anybody?"

"He doesn't know."

"Oh."

I said, "He ran a mortar squad. He probably killed a lot of people that way, but he couldn't see them. They were out in the bush."

"Oh."

One of the Marines on TV quit kissing the woman he was with and started talking to her and crying.

Will said, "I think my daddy killed some people he could see."

For the Marines on TV it was back to the jungle and the war, another firefight: nighttime, tracer rounds, fallen buddies from the good times in Hawaii. It finished.

I said, "If I tell you something, you promise not to tell?"

"Okay."

"I can't even tell my mama."

"Is it gross?"

"Nuh-uh."

"Off color?"

"I don't think so."

"Why can't you tell her?"

"My daddy just said not to."

"Would he whoop you if you did?"

"Maybe."

"Does your daddy whoop you for stuff?"

"Well, yeah. Does yours?"

"My mama does."

"Does that hurt?"

"Sometimes."

"So you promise?"

"I promise."

"Okay. My daddy said he was happy when he got drafted."

We were still watching the movie, but the good parts were over, only talking left. Slow music started.

Will said, "Is that it?"

I said, "Looks like it."

He said, "No, what your daddy said not to tell."

I said, "Yeah."

"Shoot, I would've been happy too."

"Shoot, me too."

"They don't draft people anymore."

"I know."

"You got to be eighteen to be drafted."

"I know."

"I wish I was eighteen."

"Me too. I wish I was twenty."

"Lawrence is fixing to be eighteen."

Lawrence was Will's brother, a compulsive chapsticker who would sit in his car in the driveway for an hour kissing his girlfriend while Will and I spied on them through the scope mounted on his little .22 rifle.

I said, "Lucky dog."

On TV the Marine who had cried in Hawaii was

boarding an airplane to leave Vietnam for good, though he did not look particularly happy about it. The names of the actors started floating up the screen.

"Seriously," I said. "You promise?"

He said, "I promise."

He picked up the remote control.

I said, "My daddy said he enjoyed a lot of it. Said he's glad he went."

Will changed the channel.

He said, "I don't think my daddy enjoyed it very much."

IF THERE ARE CHILDREN who do not fear being sent alone, at night, to the remotest rooms of a multi-story house, I was not one of them. And I suffered this almost nightly, when after my family's post-supper idyll of stove-made popcorn and Kool-Aid and network TV in the den downstairs, my mother would bring the evening to a sudden, brutal close by sending me upstairs—two full flights in our split-level—to take a shower.

Did they wonder why I covered the distance like Carl Lewis?

And even on gaining the swiftly locked and brightly lit upstairs bathroom, I stripped and moved with an animal speed, rammed the sliding shower door shut behind me, and huddled, hen-fleshed, under the streaming water, in a terror I would also describe as animal had it not involved so much imagination: what unspeakable TV-land horror—scary clown, serial killer, devil worshiper—had already defeated the bathroom doorknob's pathetic twist-lock (a cinch with a toothpick) and even now stood studying, through the pebbled glass, my blurry, naked form?

Curious, that these fears did not present as eligible for prayer. Instead I resorted, with appreciable success, to a kind of protective mantra: *Stuff like* that *doesn't happen in a place like* this. By the former I meant the unspeakable TV-land horror studying me through the shower glass. And by the latter I believe I meant, most immediately, such a familiarly particularized shower as the one I was standing in—faithful home to our same old shampoo bottles, my faded maroon stadium cup from the State-Alabama game, several customers from Trish's Fuzzy Pumper Barbershop collected at the drain, Ben's deflated orange swim-floatie draped over the washcloth bar, the mate of which had popped on the ladder in Aunt Patsy's swimming pool, Aunt Patsy who was not my aunt at all (how would they ever explain that on TV?) but the woman who played the piano in our church and was the wife of a cotton-farming elder who wore a straw fedora and seersucker suits and kept a pipe-holder mounted on the dash of his pickup, the two of whom had a shaggy-haired son at Ole Miss who could sing and play "Peaceful Easy Feeling" on the acoustic guitar and a tree-shaded swimming pool with a water slide anybody in our church could come over and use anytime they wanted.

TV showers, by contrast, were so obviously TV showers. Starkly generic, they lacked any object or detail requiring explanation. And even when I sometimes noticed what I assumed were efforts to give a slice of TV-land the specificity that would make it seem real to somebody, somewhere, which I was willing to assume it did, those efforts did nothing for me: the things they put in to make TV-land look and sound real simply did not look or sound like the things in my real world. Where were the three-wheelers? The popped floaties? The crawdads? Nobody ever got serially killed on a TV show where boys rod-and-reeled crawdads up out of a ditch that disappeared into a snake-and-spider-infested culvert and hosted the loveliest black-and-blue dragonflies that were harder to hit with a pellet pistol than you'd think. No zombie ever burrowed up out of the soil on a program where a woman named Miss Sissy strolled up a twilit driveway through the lazy flaring of lightning bugs with a Chihuahua named Duchess fainted on her shoulder.

No, this was not a TV shower, I assured myself, we did not live in a TV town, still less a TV neighborhood, we did not talk or laugh like TV people, did not discuss TV things, did not make preposterous TV mistakes, like inviting eerily polite TV strangers into our homes to use the telephone upon hearing they were Having Car Trouble. In sum, we did not live TV lives, and we would not die TV deaths.

BECAUSE HE WAS unfailingly generous, so able and quick to follow, I could hazard an openness with Will Melancon I dared not with others. As noted, this made for moments of heady solidarity. It also, in the way of such things, raised the stakes of the inevitable disillusionment. Thus an exchange that discourages me, even now, to recall.

I was spending the night at Will's, and we were lying in his room, in twin beds, in the dark. We had been the last ones stirring in the house, and neither of us had made a sound for some minutes. But Will's room was alive with moonlight and shadows, and I had that weird feeling I often do, that something commandingly sublime and venturesome is in the air, that the world is issuing a call that must be answered, and—here is the essence of the thing—only the immoderate deed will do. It is, I am convinced, what makes the prophet preach and the roué prowl. We are brothers all, negotiating the same inkling of superabundance, the same uncontainable impulse blooming out of our hearts. Having swallowed dryly against it, I whispered:

"I think Mrs. Nettles is pretty."

Mrs. Nettles was our fifth-grade Social Studies teacher, and these were my immoderate words—unmistakable, unretractable—in the silence, in the moonlight.

They hung on the air for but a moment and vanished, unanswered.

Oh, I ached. Merely spoken, the words brought no relief. I needed them heard, gaped at, marveled on. I rolled over on my side with the pain, and nearly missed it when it came:

*"Me too."*

I snatched my head from the pillow, cut the noise of my breathing.

I whispered, "What?"

Will whispered, "Me too."

I whispered, "You think Mrs. Nettles is pretty?"

He whispered, "Yes."

My head fell back to the pillow. I breathed again.

I whispered, "I think she is so pretty."

He whispered, "Me too."

I whispered, "Her being heavyset don't bother me."

He whispered, "Me neither."

My breathing was competing with my need to swallow.

I whispered, "I think Mrs. Nettles . . . is *beautiful*."

Blood was thumping in my ears, but I heard it:

*"Me too."*

I was panting.

Will whispered, "Would you kiss Mrs. Nettles?"

I could barely manage to exhale it:

"Yeeesss."

He whispered, "What?"

I whispered, "Yes!"

He whispered, "Me too."

I whispered, "I would kiss her."

He whispered, "I would kiss Mrs. Nettles."

I whispered, "Me too."

He whispered, "Her walking like that don't bother me."

I whispered, "Me neither."

He whispered, "I would still kiss her."

I whispered, "Me too."

I tried to think of something else to whisper.

The silence threatened to swallow us.

Will whispered, "I would kiss Mrs. Nettles."

I whispered, "Me too."

But reeling with it all, I was trying to think, to feel, to reach for and find the exact right thing to say next, the thing that would duly answer what was in the night around me, that would express everything I felt and, at the same time, make me feel it more, when in the silence, in the moonlight, with irrefutable clarity, Will whispered:

"I *love* Mrs. Nettles."

Very quietly, very precisely, it killed everything. Not quite the effect of snapping on the overhead light, more like clicking on a small lamp in the corner, which, even with its unpresuming field, dispels all the magic from a moonlit room. And I blame myself. I invite, nay, require people to join me in my reaching, only to judge them and withdraw when in an honest effort they go where I—presuming to distinguish the yawp of immoderation from the sin of overreaching—refuse to follow. Or don't know how. In either case, the soul is small.

I whispered, "I would kiss Mrs. Nettles."

I no longer panted.

Will whispered, "Do you love her?"

How I hurt for him now. But, no, I did not love Mrs. Nettles. Neither did he. Mrs. Nettles had an Orkin Man husband with a broad chest and hairy forearms who sometimes brought lunch to her at school in a clamshell Styrofoam box. He knew what it was to love her. We, on the other hand, were eleven, and according to my father, when in the second grade I'd found courage at the dinner table to announce my love for a button-eyed classmate named Christie Autry, we had no idea what love is.

But what else could I say?

"Yes," I whispered. "I do."

Will whispered, "Me too. I *luuuuv* her."

I whispered, "Yeah."

He whispered, "Ohhhhhh."

I whispered, "What?"

"Ohhhhhh," Will cooed. "Ohhhhh, I *luuuuv* Mrs. Nettles . . . ."

I rolled over, and covered my ears.

SOME PEOPLE resemble their pets, others their vehicles. Mr. Melancon drove an undersized, dingy-white, foreign-make pickup. This little machine twittered and buzzed in a visceral, private labor when taking the hills in and out of the neighborhood, collected dead leaves, broken tools, aluminum cans when it sat in the driveway. A joyless dissent of a vehicle. Naturally, I attached to it the foreboding I held for Mr. Melancon, and I could no more imagine riding in it than I could imagine slipping my bare feet into his moccasin house shoes.

Then came the night I rode in it.

Will and I were in the sixth grade, and my mother had dropped us off at the Pizza Hut out on the highway for dinner. It was an early experiment in our independence, and we had a high, stupid-funny time of it, plundering the breadstick bucket at the salad bar, hooting and high-fiving over the Ms. Pac-man, snorting powdered parm off our pinky tips, blow-gunning bits of wet napkin and crushed ice through our straws, barely touching our pizza. I said, "You want to see if I can spend the night?" Will said, "Yeah!" We got his mother on the pay phone. She said yes. We got my mother on the pay phone, told her what his mother said. My mother said yes. We got his mother on the pay phone again. His daddy would be there in ten minutes.

Through the plate-glass window of our booth I caught sight of the little truck as it came coasting down the dark ramp from the highway and leveled into the sparely lit parking lot. And as I watched it came gliding through the pools of shadow to pass directly beneath the light under the eave outside our window, so that Mr. Melancon's face inside the cab was, for the space of a camera flash, both close and visible. Something in his expression arrests me still. For one thing, it was the discomfitingly transparent face of a man who supposed himself to be unobserved. But there was something more, something I find difficult not merely to phrase, but to apprehend. Here, after all, was just another serious-faced man, in another dirty truck, in another obscure little town, as complete a cipher as ever wandered and died upon the baked-mud plains of prehistory. And yet, had someone managed to call your attention to the expression on that face so briefly visible amid the shadows, I believe you might very well have sat forward for a closer look, and thought, *Well, yeah, now that you mention it . . . .* So I will try to say it: he looked amazed to the point of exhaustion on finding himself in the middle of some man's life, and utterly unable to believe it was his.

On the highway home, the cab of the pickup was cramped and dreamy with green dashlight. It was also pungent with what I recognized to be beer breath. Mr. Melancon drove with his eyes fixed firmly on the road. He had the radio off, and had not spoken to us.

I said, "They usually put doo-doo on them."

Meaning punji sticks. A continuation of our dinner discussion.

Will was sitting between Mr. Melancon and me, staring at the quivering green pommel of the gear shift.

He said, "I know."

I said, "To cause infection, to spread disease."

He said, "Yeah."

I said, "Because, when you think about it, what's worse: getting killed all the sudden, like getting your head blown off, or getting a deep nasty puncture wound that gets infected, like in your foot, or maybe your testicles, so you die real slow and painful?"

Will nodded, by which I took him to mean a deep nasty puncture wound that gets infected so you die real slow and painful.

I said, "They were smart that way."

Will nodded again.

We rode in silence.

I could hear Mr. Melancon breathing long and slow through his nose, like someone sleeping, but I could see he was fully awake, saw him blink. After a while, he cleared his throat.

He said, "Your daddy shot mortars?"

I said, "Yessir."

Mr. Melancon nodded, watched the road.

I said, "He led a mortar squad."

Mr. Melancon nodded again.

I said, "He was on Vung Chua Mountain."

I thought he might know it.

Mr. Melancon did not appear to consider whether he might know it. He just kept breathing long and slow through his nose, eyes on the road.

Finally, he said, "Your daddy made the mess, and I had to look at it."

Whatever I did not understand about this remark, I understood it was not friendly.

Mr. Melancon said, "I had to walk around in it. Pick through it. I doubt your daddy had to do that."

I knew my daddy had in fact seen a mess or two. True, his main job had been to provide mortar support from the base on the mountain, but he had gone on patrols through the jungle like everybody else. He had been there when McElvoy shot himself in the face with his grease gun. He had once even pulled the charred bodies of several South Vietnamese officers from the wreckage of a prop plane that went down on a neighboring mountain and received a certificate for it from the South Vietnamese government that he finally got translated by the woman who ran an award-winning Asian restaurant in our town. But none of this occurred to me to say. And even if it had, I believe it would have struck me as inapposite.

Mr. Melancon said, "Your daddy, he's doing all right now, huh."

"Yessir" did not feel like the right thing to say. And I couldn't think of anything else.

Mr. Melancon lifted his near hand from the steering wheel, Will moved his knee, and Mr. Melancon downshifted to take the turn into our neighborhood.

He said, "Seem like he's doing all right, I reckon."

In the dark of the Melancons' driveway, the little pickup clattered to silence. The three of us climbed out and went inside the house. Will's mother had gone to work, and his brother was not around. In the kitchen, Will and I left his daddy shuffling around in his house shoes and tucked-in undershirt and went down to the basement to shoot pool.

I have partaken in cheerier contests. But we had shut the door at the foot of the stairs, and gradually the strain began to ease. We soon recovered our pleasure in the evening. When in our second game Will blew an easy combo on the eight ball for an early win, we both threw our heads back and cried, "Ohhhh!"

I said, "Come on, man! Today's the first day of the rest of your life!"

He said, "I know! I know!"

I shook my head.

I said, "Boy hidy . . . ."

He said, "Wait, what?"

I shook my head.

I said, "Boy hidy . . . ."

He said, "No, I mean about the rest of my life."

I said, "Today's the first day of the rest of your life, man! Come on!"

He said, "What does that mean?"

I finished taking my shot, shrugged.

I said, "I don't know, John Dixon's mama has it on a magnet on their refrigerator. I think it's just supposed to encourage you."

He said, "Oh," and looked like he might say something else, but then the narrow stair from the kitchen began to squeak, after which the basement door opened, and Mr. Melancon scuffed in, carrying a plastic ashtray and a can of beer.

We paused to see if he wanted anything from us, or had just come down to get something, or what. But he didn't say anything, didn't look at us, just scuffed over to one of the darkened corners of the basement and came back dragging a tall wooden stool across the concrete floor, reentering the yellow light of the fixture that hung over the pool table. He set the stool against the wall at the rack-end of the table, took a seat on it, and lit a cigarette. He blew the smoke out his nostrils, looked at the pool table through it.

It was Will's shot. He stepped to the table, went up on his toes to stretch out across the felt, miscued, and stepped away.

I stepped to the table, miscued, and stepped away.

Mr. Melancon tapped his cigarette in his ash tray.

When Will stepped to the table, stretched out, and miscued again, Mr. Melancon just kept watching the table through his smoke. But I decided that was probably enough of that, and stepping to the table this time, settled on an improbable bank.

After blowing two clear shots on the eight ball, Will finally sunk it and took the game. The longest in my life.

Mr. Melancon stood from the stool, set his beer on it.

"Well, we got us a winner," he said, and started pulling the balls out from underneath the table and racking them on the felt. He left his cigarette in his mouth while he did this, ignoring the smoke runneling up his face, and when he had finished rolling and snugging the balls in the rack, he gently lifted it off the felt, twirled it once between his palms, and handed it to me. He took the cue from my other hand and went back to his stool to chalk it.

Will was standing against the wall at the other end of the table.

Mr. Melancon glanced down there at him, went back to chalking his cue.

He said, "Winner breaks, son."

Will stepped up and spotted the cue ball.

The break was quiet, nothing fell.

Mr. Melancon then stepped to the table with his cigarette in his lips and an unfamiliar smartness to his movements, suddenly not at all like a man in an undershirt and house shoes. After studying the table briefly, he bore down on the cue ball—his stance, his form, the very gestalt of him was smooth, assured, lovely—and drilled it. It smacked and rocketed a stripe against the back of a corner pocket, and drew perfectly on another stripe. Mr. Melancon stepped around the table, chalking his cue without looking at it, and hammered that stripe home. He went on this way, passing us in silence around the table, not taking his eyes from it, chalking his cue and squinting against his smoke while the pocketed balls thundered and rolled in the chute beneath, went on this way through the remainder of his stripes, but then left himself snookered on the eight ball and could not make the shot. Will took his time looking the table over, and when he missed his shot, Mr. Melancon stepped back in and rammed the eight ball home. He went to his stool for his beer.

"Best of three," he said.

Will leaned his cue against the wall, racked, took up his cue again, but this time didn't get to use it.

"Best of five," Mr. Melancon said, and Will racked again, and again did not shoot.

"Me against both of you," Mr. Melancon said, and this time I racked, but we never got to shoot, and when it was over Mr. Melancon took his beer from the stool, handed me his cue, and walked out of the basement, closing the door behind him.

We stood looking at the balls left on the table.

The basement stair had finished squeaking. The house beyond was still.

I said, "You want to watch MTV or something?"

Will leaned his cue against the wall. He stepped to the table, started herding the balls down it.

"You break," he said.

THAT NIGHT, from his twin bed, in the dark, his voice came just above a whisper.

"I told my daddy about your daddy."

There was no moonlight, no magic, only the dark.

I said, "It's okay."

We were silent.

He said, "But I didn't tell what I promised not to."

I still feel an affection for that boy I am hopeless to express. And though I cannot honestly say what I answered him that night, or whether I answered him at all, I am praying, with some reason to believe, I said:

"I know."

NO SNOW charmed the sodden yards as I climbed the street to the Melancons'. And in the residual chill, a tepid, rain-scented breeze licked my face, intimating stretches of time and distance that sapped my sense of self, and left me groping, vast and hollow inside. Was I truly just a boy? Or, by some trick, a man going old and gray? As well to answer: yes.

Which contributed to what was already a disquietingly strange walk up the hill. For one thing, with every step I had taken, my loose sense of intention seemed gradually to have solidified into some firmness of purpose that, nevertheless, remained obscure. Just what was I so determined to do? And what, for that matter, had determined me? Genuine sympathy? The allure of an exhortation that verged on poesy? Chance recollections, of Will, of Mr. Peterson? But I'm not certain, even now, I can reliably distinguish between these possibilities.

Stranger yet, however, was a confounding blindness in my memory, as perverse as the one that claimed Miss Sissy, and if possible more repellent: while I knew I must have been in Will's company many times since the night his father drove us home from the Pizza Hut, I could not, for the life of me, recall anything about such an occasion. Not a single specific thing we had talked about, laughed at, done together. Indeed, to this day I can recall nothing about being with Will again, ever, after that night, though I know we remained friendly through high school. Nor do I remember hearing what he did or where he went after graduating. And in all the years between then and the day I chanced to hear what became of him as still so young a man, I never once thought of taking the no-trouble to look him up. A capacity for indifference I will own, and for which I maintain a low-grade distaste. But that, of all occasions, the night made so grimly luminous by his father should be the boundary of my memory of him, the suggestion that from precisely then I, someone I have always been, was no longer able or willing to follow so fine a friend, so kind a boy—this is the stuff of disgust, of despair.

Add to all this that when at last I reached the Melancons' driveway and looked up at their house and yard, I got surprised by an unwelcome impression: the one you have on returning, as an adult, to one of the momentous places of your childhood—a school you attended, the house you grew up in, a pond you used to fish—to find it so much smaller and shabbier than you remember, though it may yet throb with poignance. In this case, that place was the home of my friend Will Melancon: uselessly tiny front yard, weeds standing in the cracked walk, warped siding and blistered trim, rust and belly in the window screens, in the driveway a small, tarped vehicle on blocks. And I stood there, at the foot of the drive, asking that question you invariably have: was it always like this?

I went up the walk, mounted the front step, stood listening to the overgrown holly hedge rasp in the wind. There was no other sound from the house.

I pressed the doorbell button, and waited.

I rapped on the storm door glass, and waited.

I pulled open the storm door, and was reaching for the dull brass knocker when the lock on the wooden door clacked, the seal at the jamb sucked free, and the wooden door drew slowly open.

A pitiably reduced Mr. Melancon—stubble-headed, saggy-throated, eyes loose-rimmed and watery—stood in the half-open door, plaid flannel hanging unbuttoned over his undershirt, and blinked at me. Only eventually with recognition. He then looked over my shoulder, out to the street, the neighborhood beyond, as though for the first time in a long while, then took in the sight of me again. At last he gave a small nod, less in welcome, I'd say, than concession.

I followed him through the familiar but no longer especially tidy living room, into a window-lit kitchen gone dim with the coming of a storm. There he eased himself onto his same old stool, at his same old spot at the serving counter, and without raising his eyes, motioned me around opposite. I stepped around, and pulled out the stool there.

Neither of us had yet spoken, and some aspect of the situation, some indistinct declaration in his manner, said he would do so first. But he was in no hurry. And while we sat there, he studied me. Unable to return his gaze, I settled mine on the countertop—perennial molded-plastic ashtray, water glass—and listened for the sound of anyone else in the house. There was only the hissing of the trees out back, a soft thunder rumbling in.

Mr. Melancon sighed, as if impatient.

But I did not know what to do about it.

Finally, he said, "I reckon you know about Will."

It is here I come closest to giving this up.

What an impossible moment I have contrived.

For what, God help me, should I say I knew?

Maybe that I always knew something was scary wrong.

Maybe that I knew he might well begin this way.

Certainly that, all the same, I had no answer for it.

And I am sorry to say, for now, I simply nodded.

BUT WITH THIS I was able to look up from the counter at him, and I saw I was wrong, there was no impatience. Instead, with his hands in his lap and his shoulders rolled forward, the man looked so burdened in mind and body he could barely sit upright. Yet he had not stopped studying me.

"You look afraid," he said.

I could not think of anything to say.

He said, "What is it you're afraid of?"

His tone was not hostile, in fact almost tender, his question a sincere invitation. And reaching for the determination I had felt in the street when climbing the hill, I made myself return his stare.

"You," I said.

I did not expect him to be offended, but I did expect him to ask me why, and I was already searching for the honest answer when he dismissed what I had said with a shake of his head, leaned slowly forward to rest his forearms on the edge of the counter, and fixed me with all the burden in his eyes.

"No," he said. "I mean, what are you *really* afraid of?"

What strikes me is how readily I understood the question, and how willing I was to consider it. Indeed, I wanted very badly to answer it, if for no other reason than that I felt I owed it to someone I sensed was trying to help me. But in the end I could not. Maybe I was too distracted by the circumstances. Maybe I was not smart enough, or honest enough. Or maybe there is something infinitely elusive at the heart of the question, like when you try to imagine the length of eternity.

"I don't know," I said finally.

Mr. Melancon leaned back from the counter, reached out and tipped the plastic ashtray to look inside, the way you unconsciously inspect the grounds in the bottom of a coffee cup. Rain had begun pelleting the windows, and I had to strain to hear him.

He said, "But something."

I said, "Yes, sir. I think so."

He went on looking in the ashtray, and after a moment he nodded.

He said, "Me too."

Whatever I was really afraid of, I no longer feared him.

I said, "What do you think it is?"

He left the ashtray alone. Shook his head.

He said, "I don't know, son."

He brought his hands back to his lap. Took a deep breath. Again shook his head.

He said, "I don't know either."

Sheets of rain were blowing against the side of the house. A stretch of thunder rolled, went jingling through the glassware in the cabinets. In the lull after, he cleared his throat.

"I used to figure it was just the worst thing I could think to happen," he said.

He stopped himself from reaching for the ash tray.

He said, "I guess that's not it."

Can I do this?
*Soothe the suffering.*
*Pity the afflicted.*
Mr. Peterson would.
Mr. Peterson would try.

I swallowed.

"Would it help you," I said, "to talk about Will?"

For a moment he did not move, did not blink. He seemed to have gone very far away, and I wondered whether he had heard me. But then he looked down the counter, to the uncurtained window there. A huddled, wet-eyed animal seeking aperture, light.

"Maybe so," he said.

His eyes reflected the rainy light from the window. His voice required effort to find.

He said, "But probably all I can tell you about is me."

We sat again in silence while he went on looking at the window. A tic played in his face. I could see he was waiting, measuring, did not trust his voice. At last he took a quick breath.

"I had so much—" was all he got out before the spasm twisted his face, and I saw him try, hideously, to race it, this thing welling up within him, stealing his body, his voice.

"I couldn't see him . . ." is what I think he said, and he shook his head in a futile pleading with the thing that was overtaking him, raised his hands to present the empty air across the counter beside me, ". . . right there— for years—and I couldn't . . . ," and his face and hands went on working, but not his voice.

I jumped when he slammed the counter.

And having come to his feet, he took himself to the spattered, softly ticking window, turned his back to me, and cried.

As I watched him stand there with his head down, shoulders shaking, making no noise amid the gentle rhythms of the tapering rain, yet another insoluble math bloomed within me, so that I felt with my whole and swelling heart I should say something—and I was willing, willing to say anything at all, as I was willing now to hear anything—but at the same time and perfectly apace felt nothing would serve, that the more desperately I wanted to say something the less any particular thing would do, desire would ever outrun possibility, because even if to some non-negligible degree I apprehended this man's suffering, it was, finally, only apprehension, and not what was apprehended: to mean anything, *we* must remain divisible by *you* and *I*.

Mr. Melancon had lifted his face again to the window. His shoulders had stopped shaking. He ran the back of his hand across his mouth. Sniffed.

"I love him," he said to the glass. "I loved him always."

I don't have to know, but maybe that was what I had come for, what I was there to hear, and credit. This ravaged man's love for the little boy with the thin bangs and puffing sigh, penchant to miscue and a dimpled belly, a soul so able and quick to follow. My friend Will Melancon was a soldier's son who grew up and gave his life for his country, meeting his end and his beginning in what, for me, will almost certainly remain the forever-far mountains of Afghanistan. And when I imagine his father, stirred reluctantly from his stool by a doorbell, scuffing from the kitchen at a pace that lacked any regard for the ensuing rap at the storm glass, taking his own time to unlock and pull open that wooden front door . . . on a pair of unsmiling strangers in dress blues, asking for him by his full name and with that chilling courtesy they do rather well on TV, I am certain he knew it all, in every detail that mattered, before they said another word.

# Ars Longa, Dies Brevis

IF IN THE SPRINGTIME of my boyhood you had turned off the highway onto the loud rock macadam or (later) plush quiet blacktop, climbed through the stands of pine and hardwood between road cuts concealed in kudzu, come round the bloom-blind turns and dropped then down the long hill that did not bottom until you crossed the bridge, and on that bridge had seen a boy, leaning on the guardrail, gazing on the sun-baked rocks, the glittery mud, the slow and buggy water, it could have been me, or any one of thirty boys I would have called, at one time or another, my neighbor. Many yet unmentioned I began to find in the street and yards on leaving the Melancons', with the tonic scent of the departed rain rising fresh from the grass, the mild fire of the sun leveling through the treetops, and the fearlessness I had attained in the presence of Mr. Melancon a solid thing within me. The first I met was standing in the gutter at the end of the drive, watching the pollen suds roil over his shoes.

Richie Wiggins was a pale, daft, fireplug of a boy who grew up and committed suicide. He was not unintelligent, but unnervingly opaque, the sort of child who appeared exceedingly pleased at odd moments and was perhaps too easily talked into playing the cumbersome, disrespected instruments in bands. Bass guitar. Bari sax. "Tuba," intoned Mr. Harding, our irritable band director whose patchy beard did not hide the pink seams of youthful indiscretion on a motorcycle, "let's hear your line. One and two and . . . ," and whether it was Richie, or what had been written for his instrument, I would never have recognized it as music. Though Mr. Harding, ever to my surprise, always seemed fine with it.

Richie would turn up in the neighborhood at random intervals, come from out in the county to live "in town" awhile with his grandparents, a withdrawn old pulpwooder and the wife of his youth whose house sat back up in the woods, out of sight, down an unpaved tentacle off the development. At school, for whatever reason, I never saw much of Richie. But when he lived with his grandparents, we rode the same bus home (it let him out in the street, just past Sam MacBride's, to walk the gravel tentacle), and on these rides he was indiscriminately sociable, to the point of growing hoarse and damp-headed with sweat. One afternoon the frustrated gladiatrix who drove our bus with a short-handled boat paddle within reach on the dash looked up in the rearview mirror and growled at Richie to turn around, sit down, and be quiet, please sir, how about it. Richie obliged her just long enough to smile back at her in the mirror, pull a three by five index card from his shirt pocket, and hold it up for her to see: it had NO, THANK YOU written on it. Richie then repocketed the card and sprang from his seat to join another conversation. To this day, it remains one of the deftest, most strangely satisfying things I have ever seen.

But what came immediately to mind when I heard that, as a thirty-two-year-old man, Richie Wiggins had taken his life with a handgun was the afternoon he crashed a Two-Below football game in my front yard and demanded to be tackled. To clarify: we often played tackle, particularly when the game was Roughhouse, that one-against-all affair in which one boy stands with his back to the others, tosses the ball over his head like a bridal bouquet, and whoever catches it takes off with everyone in pursuit until they grab him and pile on and ride him to the ground, after which he gets up, stands with his back to the others, tosses the ball over his head like a bridal bouquet, and so on, until somebody cries or gets in a fight or can't stand up or see very well anymore. But when we craved the more sophisticated, elegant, collaborative aspects of the sport—when we wanted to huddle, run plays, throw passes—we typically chose up teams and went Two Below, more effetely known among some as Two-Hand Touch Below the Waist. The device saved time and energy and, especially to the point, facilitated a certain shift of focus: from cracking bones and bloody meat and into-the-cannon's-mouth courage, to skill, athleticism, outright pleasure.

Which evidently did not interest Richie. The first time he got his hands on the ball that afternoon he stashed it under his arm like a load of stove wood, lowered his sweaty head, and started chasing his own teammates, the rest of us, everybody, all over the yard. We fled as before a disease, shouting over our shoulders at this stumpy-legged boy with the bull's frons and strange motivations to stop, man, it was Two Below! When we could no longer deny that a new event was in progress, we took turns cutting across his path like rodeo clowns, until the artless and over-animated Sidney Sizemore, desperate for promotion in our eyes, was able to get an angle on Richie, swoop in from behind, and pop him below the waist. "Got him!

Got him! I got him!" Sidney screamed, as some of us began to risk our best casual walk, but it did not work, and again we fled. Mercifully, at last, Richie wandered of his own inscrutable volition into an endzone, where he began to celebrate, humming and chuckling as he waltzed in graceful circles, hands on his leather partner's laced waist, impervious to our screaming that nuh-uh! nuh-uh! it was TWO BELOW! "Touchdown," Richie assured his dance partner, and waltzed on. What were we to do? We quit the yard and left them to it. Sidney Sizemore said, "Who-who-who the devil invited that kid anyway?"

On meeting him at the foot of the Melancons' driveway, his pale face an uncanny orange in the golden-hour sun, I asked Richie what he was doing.

He said, "Now?"

I said, "Yes."

He looked down at his shoes—bloated, gurgling, clotted with pollen—and back up at me.

He said, "Waiting on Jeff Coker."

Jeff Coker was a scrawny, strutty, foul-mouthed boy I barely knew during his brief sojourn among us, but whose very physique seemed marked for a scuzzy, bigoted manhood—bulging eyeballs, no chin, blunt thumbs. It didn't help he was a cousin of Harlan Grubb's.

I said, "What are y'all going to do?"

"I don't know." Richie shrugged. "Find something to tear up? Kill something?"

I said, "Bring Jeff and y'all come to the bridge in thirty minutes."

He said, "I thought you didn't like Jeff."

I said, "He ain't my favorite."

He said, "Mine neither."

I said, "But I'm trying."

He said, "Tell me about it."

The bloodless ball of Richie's fist flew up before his face.

He said, "Synchronize watches?"

He sported an old-school analog on a leather cuff band. Very Elvis Presley. It suited Richie exactly, and I was happy for him. But with a glance at the treetops, I told him my eye was on the sun. Then set off down the hill, at a trot.

THEY SAY you can't make this stuff up. But I'm sitting with Zeke and John Dixon on a spongy log among the willows, down below the white-clapboard, achingly silent house, in the time of plentiful bream. We're done eating, and before us sits a Styrofoam minnow bucket, the water in it a kaleidoscope of silver and purple.

John Dixon says, "These minners are happy. Sometime they sell you agitated minners."

Zeke snorts.

He says, "You don't know they're happy. You ain't a minner."

John Dixon says, "Well, you ain't me. You don't know what I know."

Zeke says, "I know I'm more like you than you are them minners."

John Dixon yawns. Turns and lies back along the log, pulls his cap down over his eyes.

"I don't know," he says. "You sound kind of agitated to me."

DOWN THE HILL and across the bridge, breathless, I jogged up Brunson and Spencer Willet's long, curving drive, to find a wiffle ball game in their backyard. The Willet brothers often hosted these in the ample grassy plot between their back patio and their grandfather Peepaw's trailer. Neither brother excelled at the sport, but it did allow them to showcase a shared passion for heckling, clowning, and irksome pranks—home plate was a garden hose coiled on the grass, you came up to bat, they'd turn on the hose, that sort of thing.

Brunson, the younger, was in the tenth grade and already town-famous for his drum majoring. He had a skinny neck and enormous hair, and though not especially athletic, he had rhythm in every joint and was fantastically limber. People with no interest in our mediocre high school football team would crowd the bleachers on a Friday night just to see Brunson swagger out to mid-field at half-time in his plumed helmet, high collar, and epaulettes, ready Freddie to do his thing: an obligatory prelude of whistle-blowing and mace-twirling that, gradually, under the weight of a palpably rising tension in the stadium, gave way to a fury of high-stepping, long-stomping, air-wading, hip-juking, shoulder-rolling, roboting (best in the world), now snapping his chin up, down, and all around, as though looking for something only a boy who's lost his cotton-picking mind would look for, and ending—always, but never when you expected it—in a violent plunk on the grass in full splits, all of Brunson frozen but for the heaving in his tunic, helmet fallen forward over his eyes, face set in stone for the roaring stands. On my feet and cheering, I told everyone who could hear me this was my across-the-street neighbor, very nice guy, maybe not the best at wiffle ball, etc.

The older brother, Spencer, had just graduated from high school, sizable, loutish, and pock-faced. In virtually every memory I have of him he is laughing, but about him and his laughter there is something reachy and uncouth. When this large, older boy looked you in the eyes, his swam. When he laughed with you, you had the uneasy sense y'all might not be laughing at the same thing. And this was well before the neighborhood mothers began to spot him at the mall in Jackson, two hours away, dressed in women's clothing. Certainly long before I heard he had moved off (that crowded, adverb of a place) to die of AIDS. So while I will admit it is hard not to exaggerate or sentimentalize the look in the swimmy eyes of the teenage Spencer Willet I knew, I still say it was the look of someone incessantly distracted, if not intoxicated, by the thought that chaos just might be the one true God.

I stood on the Willet brothers' back patio, catching my breath, sizing up the game, getting anxious about the time. But these were all much older boys, and I balked at interrupting. Here was six-foot-three Oscar Arnold, known for his affability and manners; Brother Jim Keller's twin sons, not so much; Stevie Taylor, who with his spidery fingers would take second place in Hal & Mal's Best Guitar Player in the Magnolia State contest; his older brother Mike Jr. Taylor, who with his spidery fingers was a savant of small engine repair; and Daniel McClintock, a pudgy hobbit with a full beard and permanent grin that kept his eyes from opening all the way. For the time being, then, I waited for a break in the action, and kept a restive check on the sun.

While I waited, Peepaw Willet came puttering up the driveway in the faded red Datsun pickup he drove only when drunk, and from which he would soon be ejected through the windshield to die on the cracked white pavement of Old Highway 3. In this conveyance he now trundled across the Willets' backyard, through the middle of the wiffle ball game, observing us out his open window with the air of a debauched potentate drawn by horses, peering without expression at whoever happened into view, ruminatively smacking his gums. He had a face like a roasted nut and wore a baggy cloth cap like you see in old photographs of people you're meant to feel sorry for. On exiting the far side of the wiffle ball game, the pickup cornered Peepaw's trailer, out of my sight, where the motor soon died with a cough, a clank, a snuffle, which hadn't quite finished when the pickup door croaked open.

Just then Spencer slapped a pitch from Brunson over everybody's head, into the next yard, and took off tearing around the bases, stifling an undignified grunt-laugh like somebody getting away with something cruel. He barreled around first base with those farthest afield still chasing after the ball, swept past second, stamped a foot on the trailer step that was third, and had started for coiled-garden-hose home when, at last, the relay came in from the next yard, Brunson fielded it clean, yelled "You're dead, son!" and while Spencer turned his head, drew up his shoulders, and squealed, Brunson hauled off with the hard-plastic wiffle ball and drilled him square in the back, scoring the sound of raw meat shot with an air rifle. Side retired.

I stepped onto the grass.

I said, "Hey, y'all, I think everybody's meeting at the bridge."

Spencer had his shirt off, trying to see the red whelp on his hairy back.

He said, "We're playing a game."

Six-foot-three Oscar Arnold said, "You want in?"

One of Brother Jim Keller's twins said, "He's little."

The other one said, "Y'all can have him."

Brunson said, "Peepaw!" and took off running toward the trailer.

When we reached the faded red Datsun, the bottom half of Peepaw lay in the driver's side floorboard and the rest of him was hanging out onto the grass, trying to finish throwing up. He was calm about it, mostly just working his tongue and lips with the small, sticky sounds of an infant. Brunson and Oscar Arnold stooped and took him gently under the armpits. Spencer guffawed, turned to me.

"How is he not dead yet?" he said.

I tracked the eyes wandering back and forth in the vicinity of mine.

I glanced at the westerly treetops, the pinkening sky.

In a tone meant to be as respectful as possible of the circumstances, I said, "Y'all try to come to the bridge."

TOO OFTEN I HAPPEN on vital moments long forgotten. Sitting cross-legged, say, on a floor of pin oak leaves before a tinplate lunch box, sucking grape Kool-Aid, never quite sweet enough, through the spout of a thermos inside which the ice no longer clatters, only clicks, because it's melting. Or thigh-deep in the shallows of the Angel's Pond, shouting and laughing and splashing with John Dixon in pursuit of a long red thread, our stringer, pulled loose from the bank by our only fish now making for deeper water, the two of us chasing and grabbing at it through the mats of slime-green scum, the summer stink of the water flying up in our faces, the warmth of it on my cheek, in my mouth . . . . And when I am done with the memory, or it with me, and I have returned to the so-called Here and Now, I am subject to brood on the tyranny of the latter, to darken on the possibility that, given the pace and profluence of even the slowest life, it may well be that I never have that memory again. I am not above jotting the quick reminder—*picnics under pin oaks . . . red stringer with JD . . .* —but I am not always within reach of a pencil.

I've tried preserving some of these in stories. Drafts and redrafts in odd notebooks, on loose pages. But I can't say it satisfies. I have mentioned the door that closes in the effort to bring a memory into words. And then there is the hassle and distraction of relevance. Does it matter to my story how it felt on school-day mornings, sitting on the kitchen counter in front of the window that gives a view through the carport and down the drive to the empty stretch of street where, periodically, cars I recognize appear from behind the low hill on the vacant lot, appear and float past our drive without a tinge of pertinence until suddenly everything is different, because from behind the low hill of the vacant lot has appeared the square, butter-colored snout of Mrs. Barry's Oldsmobile, and there is that long, long fraction of a second when I watch it with my whole being, to detect whether they have remembered, whether the car is slowing, whether its object is our driveway—is, in fact, me—and the quick, deep (so long forgotten!) pinch of pleasure when I can tell—*yes!*—it is slowing, now more noticeably, now almost to a stop, is now taking the turn into our driveway, the wide, chrome grill-snout yawing around, rising from its dip through the gutter with a distant tire-crackle as the gleaming body of the car straightens toward me, to come nosing up the drive, gliding in under my basketball goal, where it stops, with the impenetrable glare of the sky on its windshield?

But far worse, for telling stories, is something like the opposite difficulty. Where I lose any faith in *irrelevance*. Where in pursuit of a particular, seemingly distinct memory, I find instead only an opening into another, and another, none more complete, more terminal, than the one before, and losing any effectual sense of their separateness I am drawn down a vortex of Memory, where there is no discernible narrative shape, no discernible logic, and relevance is like light trapped in a shoebox lined with aluminum foil. Everything is meaningful. Everything is now. But I have left anything I recognize to be the coherence of Story far behind, have lost even the necessary assumptions of Time and the Self, and there is only the terrible question, the burden, of what to do with it all. At such times I physically ache to tell a story, but cannot find the distinctions that make it possible. Or having already pre-sumed to begin one, lose hope of remaining intelligible.

JOGGING AWAY from the pietà over Peepaw Willet, I came upon Anthony Williams and his father and their crew simultaneously mowing, weed-eating, edging, and raking the elderly Jenkins' big, beautiful yard. Anthony and his father and their crew were black. They wore lemon-yellow T-shirts and wide-brimmed hats. Which looked like a costume on Anthony because I was used to seeing him at school, where he made good if irregular money giving chess lessons at recess, wore collared shirts in muted tones, and went bare-headed. Not to suggest he was at all dull or retiring. He was in fact passably athletic and incorrigibly mischievous and had a quick, subtle humor wed with a throaty, grown-man laugh that yanked his head back. He was also an easy, gamesome companion. On the kickball diamond our high-fives were frequent and heartfelt, in the cafeteria line our conversation by turns bust-a-gut and melancholy. It was Anthony who told me Marvin Gaye's own father had dragged him out of the shower and stabbed him to death with a butcher knife, which proved wrong in its particulars but remains notable for being the first I heard Marvin *fils* was dead.

I'd never realized, however, that Anthony's father was the B.B. Williams of B.B. Williams Lawn and Garden Service, whose shiny pickups and flatbed trailers were pulled up at curbs all over town, until one summer day a detachment of B.B. Williams men arrived in our neighborhood to deploy over the elderly Jenkins' front yard, where soon after, chancing to pass in the street, I recognized Anthony among them. He was raking clippings. I hollered, "Anthony!" He looked up and smiled. We waved. And in an edifying dumbshow of mutual courtesy, during which his father too looked up at me, smiled, and waved, Anthony got permission to come play. We shot basketball in my driveway. My mother said, "Hey, Anthony!" and brought out glasses of lemonade on a tray. Anthony pushed the brim of his hat up out of his eyes and took a long swig. He brought the glass down and went, "Ahhhh." He said, "Thank you very much." My mother said, "You're so welcome." I said, "Mama, Anthony's helping mow the Jenkins' yard." She said, "Yes!" We shot more basketball. I said, "You want to see if you can spend the night?" He said, "Yeah!" We parted to get the necessary permissions—he from across the street, I from inside—and met again in my driveway. He said,

"I gotta go." I said, "Me, too." He said, "See you at school." I said, "You know that's right." He said, "Dap"— we brushed palms, fingers.

Now a couple of years older, stouter, quieter, Anthony came walking down the elderly Jenkins' driveway wearing a turned-off weed-eater on a shoulder strap. He looked handsomely martial with his chest puffed out, his lemon-yellow T-shirt peppered with grass clippings. I waited for him at the foot of the drive, against the fender of one of his father's trailers.

When he got there, I said, "What's up, Anthony."

He set the weed-eater on the trailer, lifted his chin.

He said, "Sup."

I said, "Not too much." I said, "A bunch of us are meeting at the bridge." I nodded down the street at it. "Think you can come?"

He was unscrewing the cap on the weed-eater's gas tank. He shook his head.

He said, "I gotta trim this yard. Maybe some other time."

He took up a milk jug of gas and oil, checked the top was on good.

*How to put this?*

I said, "Thing is, well, this might be the only time."

Anthony was shake-blending the contents of the jug.

"Well, now, that's y'all on that," he said. "But I can't, man. Not today."

He filled the tank on the weed-eater, put the jug away, clipped the weed-eater back on the strap, ran the strap across his puffed-out chest like a bandoleer.

All the while I stood there watching him, staying out of his way, like a small child watching his father dress for work, and tried to think how to explain myself, how to make this make sense, not without some doubt that it did.

He said, "I tell you what."

I said, "What."

He said, "I got a bridge in *my* neighborhood. Y'all can come over there any time."

I looked at Anthony.

He looked at me. He lifted his eyebrows.

Yes, absolutely—I cast an eye at the setting sun—this was awkward. For starters, I had no idea what neighborhood he was talking about. No idea where my easy, gamesome, incorrigibly mischievous friend Anthony lived (would they keep these trucks and trailers there?) or whom he lived with, no idea who his mother was, whether he had brothers or sisters, or what he did when he was not at school or helping his father with someone's yard. And about the only thing mitigating a sudden overwhelming sense of deficiency as his friend in this moment was recognizing I had enough sense to know it would not be okay to say, *That's a real good point, Anthony, but listen, I'm afraid I don't have time to discuss all this right now.*

I said, "Anthony, where, um . . . or who—"

But then got startled by Anthony's wide-open mouth, his head flying back, and out came that great, throaty, grown-man laugh. And while he laughed I could think of nothing to do with myself but stand there, as though in the basin of a geysering fountain, alternately shivered and soothed by the cold, sky-flung ropes that were falling to the surface—kuh-*slap*, kuh-*slap*—all around me. When at last he could, with some effort, Anthony brought his head back down and shook it to himself, still laughing.

"I'm just messing," he said.

But he could not stop shaking his head, could not stop chuckling, and as usual between us this was infectious, so that despite the distress still burning in my scalp and cheeks, I could not help laughing a little myself.

I said, "Yeah, all right."

Winding down, he dabbed each eye with a knuckle.

He sighed: "Oooeee . . . ."

He said, "Just messing."

I said, "I hear you."

He said, "Uh-huh. I believe you do."

He said, "But we'll talk about it."

I said, "I believe we will."

He then peeked over his shoulder, at the crew spread over the big yard behind him, mowing, weed-eating, edging, and raking. He leaned in, lowered his voice.

He said, "I'll slip down there in a little bit."

I said, "All right, cool."

He said, "Cool."

I said, "Dap."

Palms. Fingers. Tips.

WITH THE DOGGEDNESS of a child I learned at last how to cup my hands, align my thumbs, press their licked knuckles to my lips, and blow a low, hollow whistle. Flutter three fingers and it warbled. The eerie, wistful, wildly articulate music of TV Indians, crept in upon their enemies. Cowboy: "What was that?!" Partner: "Oh, just a bird." It did seem an improbably wonderful form of communication, suggestive of a richer and more thrilling order of brotherhood than seemed plausible, and I would not have believed it for one second had I not seen those shows with my own eyes. As it was, and having confirmed such music could indeed be made, I joined the older boys in every neighborhood raiding party, every sneaking corporate enterprise, with a single secret hope—and suffered, when invariably, without any opportunity for my music, the mission degenerated into meaningless dirt-clod battle, fist fight, cussing match, flight for cover. Until one day I got my chance. We had happened undetected upon the enemy party, huddling over their plans in the presumed safety of the Millers' shaded back patio. In we crept from the neighboring yard, through the trees and shrubbery, to semi-circle them. And having dared creep the closest, I could hear them talking, goofing, oblivious. Oh, this was it! This was perfect! I hurried to cup my hands, licked my thumbs, knelt tall in my blind—and blew. Warbled. The other party: "What was that?!" My party: "What's he doing?!" The other party: "It's them! There they are! Get 'em!"

Why was it like this?

What was wrong?

Was there a music I might learn that could save us?

I AM GENUINELY SUPRISED it doesn't cause more consternation: what does it mean to say some things really happened, some things or people are real, while others are imagined? *To imagine*, my dictionary informs, is to bring before the mind what is not present to the senses. How very little, then, is not imagined.

FARTHER ALONG the street I overtook the Harper brothers—Travis, Weems, and Little Arliss—walking one behind the other in the order of their birth. Travis, a grade ahead of me, was a thickset giant who had declared for the flute over football and wore a gold pinky ring, choices widely presumed to be difficult for his father, a hulking deputy sheriff and former All-SEC defensive tackle under Bear Bryant. Having observed their interactions at some length, however, including when Travis joined my Pee-Wee football team for the one season his father assisted our regular coach, I'd seen no evidence whatsoever to support this presumption. Weems, so cruelly saddled with preserving that distaff-side name, seemed mercifully unaffected by it. An equable fellow, he was annual Class Favorite in the grade two years behind me. Little Arliss, my sister's age, had a pronounced frontal cowlick and a deep sour streak and would go on to distinguish himself as a young man through the intoxicated destruction of public and private property (defaced buildings, totaled cars, etc.), choices I have to suppose were in fact rather inexpedient for his father.

I said, "Where y'all headed?"

They all stopped and turned.

Travis said, "We're going to the bridge."

Little Arliss looked up from scowling at the pavement, snarled, "Everybody's going," and put his head back down.

But Travis was excited. "Jeff Coker told us about it," he said.

Weems said, "Are you going, Michael?"

I said yes, but first I had to go talk to Wendy Barry.

The three of them looked at me, tilted their heads like puppies.

I had said what I said before realizing it was not something I any longer especially cared to say.

I said, "We're . . . Going together."

A light came into Travis's eyes. He said, "You and Wendy Barry are Going together?!"

I looked at Little Arliss, at Weems, at Travis.

"Well," I sighed. "Yeah."

Travis let his mouth fall open and looked all around him at the empty street. He said, "Nobody told *me*!"

I liked Travis just fine. But his indelicacy had reached the point that, had the boy been dangling from my grip this moment over some gusty black abyss, my every instinct would have been to spread all five fingers to let him plummet. That was not who I was anymore, though, I said to myself, and I did not want to go back there.

I said, "I'm not sure it's gonna work out."

Travis said, "Still! I want to hear. What's she like? She seems so . . . *mysterious*."

I could not disagree with him there. More to the point of my personal development, however, I was downright desperate not to renege on the fearlessness I had attained. Harassed and intruded upon here as I was, I could still think back and feel it, the strength in it, the freedom, the emergent taste of a defiant, invincible joy. It still seemed available to me, if only I applied myself. And I would apply myself. I would stay brave and large and open. Forever.

I said, approximately, "Travis, I do thank you for your interest. But I'm sure you will admit we don't know one another very well. Besides, I'm just not as comfortable as you are, evidently, discussing this sort of thing. I concede it may be a character flaw, and if so, I hope one day to amend it. But there it is. In the meantime, it's possible I'll have more to share when we meet at the bridge, though I do not guarantee anything and, honestly, would not hold my breath for it."

Travis's smile vanished.

His face set.

His eyes narrowed with throat-lumping intensity.

Here was, after all, a very large boy, and of a fiery lineage, and what occurred to me was that I had just invited myself into a story to be told for years to come, of that fateful afternoon in which a young Travis Harper, provoked to his life's great turning point, gave the lie to many a premature assumption on the color of his future by snatching up an impertinent neighborhood child and pounding it to death in the middle of the street.

And before I could dodge it, Travis's pinky-ringed mitt shot to my shoulder, immobilizing me. I dared not shrug it off, this heat and heft of a sirloin. All I could do was straighten my back and prepare, a stoical little pickpocket on his scaffold. Yet in these preparations, I began to reread Travis's face. The intensity there, it began to seem to me, was not that of offense, but of self-possession. And the concern that clouded it, I now saw, was for me.

"I'm sorry," he said. "I understand. I can be pushy."

Well, how about that!

I exhaled, patted the steak on my shoulder.

I said, "Thank you, Travis. Think no more of it."

So saying, I peeled away from the Harper brothers at a pretty good clip, unable to keep from smiling. Not only at remaining unpounded to death, but from a bracing sense of having cemented my recent progress.

And just in time.

The next person I meant to see, if I could, was Wendy Barry.

ARTIFICE. DECEIT. It does get tiresome. For example: what to do with the little beat-up, bored-through, written-on rock from Tucker Willingham's nightstand, back-pocketed as he came down the Willinghams' creaky upstairs hallway in a towel, tousling his hair, asking me, "What."

FEARLESSNESS, of course, is never cemented. And whatever I attained in the presence of Mr. Melancon was hardly permanent, however often and usefully I may have supposed otherwise. In younger manhood especially it smoothed the way, permitted belief in a life bedrocked on munificent reciprocity and the dividends of collective achievement. I knew days I could backslap the remotest acquaintance, take an interest in every piddling item of the broadcast news, let fly in all earnestness words like *leadership* and *community*, readily forgive the civic clubs—from Elks to Rotarians—their cornball trappings. Oh, I could be seduced to frightful commitments. Knew days I positively glowed to vote, be wed, parent.

But they never lasted. And when it would desert me, this belief, this vision, I would have no idea where it went. No precipitating crisis, I would just walk out to the car one gray morning, or step out on the sidewalk some dazzling afternoon, and realize it was not there. I could not say how, or even when, it had gone. But the intensity of its absence, not to say the increasing frequency and duration of these bouts, was such that in time I began to suspect I had only ever hoped, or pretended, to have it. Until at some point I came to see that, for whatever reason, I just may not be capable of sustaining what is necessary for it. By which I mean: believing other people exist. A little on the stagy side, but I don't know how better to say it.

Sometimes, I've noticed, when you don't understand something in a story, it's okay because there is still a lot of the story you do understand. Other times when you don't understand something in a story, it means you understand none of it.

Quite often, I find it's hard to know which is which.

IN MY DEFENSE, and to risk the persistence of the cracked, I suspect genuine belief in other people's existence is rather rare. How else to explain all the behavior on display? What else, on furthest examination, can "selfish" mean? Yes, I suspect it's where most folks (assuming they exist) lose their nerve to live like they know they ought. But we'd so much rather blah-blah about whether God exists. I say we can't be trusted with the question. What would we have Him do, step out in front of us, like a beggar on the sidewalk? Show us some tricks? Pull a universe out of a hat? Of course, the question that throws the doors open is whether I truly believe in my own existence. Or, rather, whether it makes one bit of sense for me to say either way. I mean, if it's open doors that interest.

But, hey, I don't want to give the wrong impression. I have no desire, for example, to leave off riding this sweet ol' world round and round. Mornings, especially, are pleasant. The frogs on the pond grow quiet with the coming of the light. Squirrels chatter, thump, and scrabble over the crumbling shingles. And I just lie there in the bed, or stand at one of the windows in the kitchen, and listen. Sometimes I'll walk down and take the johnboat out on the water. In the stillness of that hour the dull bump of paddle-on-gunwale carries, out of all proportion, across the open water, onto the far wooded banks, into the coves, and I like hearing it do that. When I get out near the middle I put the paddle away and just sit and drift awhile, letting the water settle, until it gets perfectly still again, and I can look down there beside the boat, on that sheet of black glass, and see me floating in the high bright clouds. Ol' Cletus, in the empyrean. One of your creepier angels. The moment I ask myself how long I plan to sit out there, I bring it in. The morning is over.

Evenings, I admit, are a different matter. Evenings are the long, bad time. The pond is noisy, bugs bomb the windowpanes, and I am not inclined to step outside, let alone leave the place. Mostly I read, or scribble a bit, and think about how there are in fact two things I would not miss, bugs and humidity. Every now and then I will pick up the soft murmuring of a motor, some lone vehicle approaching through the woods, coming carefully along the two-track from the water tower out on the highway, leaving me plenty of time to get up and kill the lights before whoever it is emerges from the trees, eases into the open grass out front, creeps there to a stop, and sits, sometimes for long minutes, sometimes much less, but all the while with the headlights streaming through the old cedars, lighting up these windows, these walls, until the visiting party does a slow three-point on the grass, and creeps back the way it came. I have discovered, rather to my surprise, I enjoy this. In those minutes when the headlights flood these windows, throwing their crazy shapes up on these walls, the night feels full to exploding with possibility. And I suppose it is. I suppose it always is.

IN THE BARRYS' unlit driveway sat a black Monte Carlo that Zeke's nine-year-old, legally blind, across-the-street neighbor, Lance Reynolds, was chasing Zeke and John Dixon around and around with a crushed squirrel from the street. Fun as it looked, I was firmly occupied. Never mind it being hard to jump in cold on something like that. Thus I gave the three of them barely a glance on my way to the porch, took a second there to catch my breath, and knocked on the Barrys' front door.

From the driveway Zeke said, "Still in her room, bet money."

I said, "I'm fixing to talk to her anyway."

He said, "I wouldn't."

I said, "That's you."

John Dixon hollered, "*Ahh-gll!* Look out!"

Zeke ducked the squirrel, side-stepped Lance.

He said, "Well, go on in, mama and daddy's at Family Night Supper."

I worked the brass latch and stepped inside.

The den glowed in lamplight. The TV was off. I eased the door to, preserving the silence, and passed through the den, soundless on the carpet. Halfway down the hall-way I stepped into the bathroom, drew a length of tissue off the roller, folded it into a neat pad.

When I reached Wendy's shut door, all was silent within. I took a deep breath. Knocked.

A rustling, and Wendy's voice:

"Who is it?"

I brought my face close to the door.

"It's me."

I stepped back. Waited. Went in close again.

"Michael."

I stepped back. Waited. Went in close again.

"Haley."

More movement within, steps on the carpet, and I thought I heard Wendy come to the other side of the door. Was that the faint sound of her breath, three inches from my face? The possibility dried my mouth. My thoughts raced. And from the soft, sudden closeness of her voice, I could tell I was right:

"What's that smell?"

I said, "Probably me."

She didn't say anything.

I said, "Michael Haley."

Still she said nothing.

I said, "Well, not really me, just some stuff that's on me: gas, possum—"

The door cracked. I retreated a step. And there, in the narrow, lighted opening, was Wendy Barry's face. Though not quite the face I had been holding before my memory's eye. It wore its usual expression of demure good humor, but had a languorous, almost sleepy cast.

Her lashes, beaded heavily with mascara, batted slowly. Her lips were un-glossed and fleshy, slightly swollen.

I said, "Mostly just gas."

She peeped past me down the hallway.

She said, "What are you doing?"

There must be a thousand ways this question can be inflected. Her way made me ask myself the same thing. And I felt how easy it would be to say that I was just checking in before taking off for the day, *so long, see you tomorrow,* and make my exit. But I held strong. I would say what I had come to say.

I said, "I have to something to say."

She assumed an obliging expression.

She said, "Okay."

I said, "I think we should Break Up."

Her obliging expression did not change.

She said, "Okay."

I offered her the pad of tissue. She looked at it through the door crack, then reached through and took it.

She said, "Thank you."

I said, "Are you okay?"

She nodded.

I said, "Are you mad?"

She shook her head.

I said, "Do you feel *scorned*?"

Her lips had moved to answer when, from behind her,

inside the room, there rose a sustained, reptilian croaking, an immense bafflement of a sound that went on long enough to invite and defeat theory after theory on its nature and source, until at last, dying, it resolved itself into the chesty timbres of human eructation, with a coda of satisfied exhalation.

Wendy and I studied one another through the door crack.

I said, "I guess that's Greg Randolph."

Her face betrayed nothing.

I said, "His car's outside."

I pictured him in there on the other side of the door, the rope chain and turtleneck, the poofy hair, the cocky, tenth-grader smile.

I said, "Plus, he just looks like somebody who'd do that."

Naturally, I said this to myself, for myself, the kind of thing you're not even sure you said out loud, but I noticed a slow, meaningful grin creep into Wendy's face, and the way she looked at me changed. I felt myself flushing. She had never looked at me like this. *Nobody* had ever looked at me like this. How was she looking at me? I would say it was like she had just this moment noticed me, only it was better than that. It was more like we both had just this moment noticed me.

"You're funny," she said.

And still grinning, still looking at me in this new way, she leaned through the crack in the door, dropped her voice to a whisper:

"He says he can't help it, he caught asthma saving somebody at the hospital."

I snorted, she shushed me, and when she did, her fingertips came up and pressed against my chest. I felt them, remaining there, while I grinned with her, or assumed I was grinning—right then hers was the only grin there was for me—and it may not have been love, but it was easily my favorite part of the whole day. And for now it was enough, though I would keep it going.

I said, "Well, I don't doubt he can't help it."

Not my best, maybe. But I had had my moment.

She took her fingers from my chest, lowered her eyes to the spot where they had rested. This was not as sultry as it sounds. Her eyebrows rose.

She said, "He did pay for half that car with his own money."

All right. Touché, Greg.

Wendy had drawn back through the crack.

"I gotta go," she said.

I said, "Me too."

I didn't go anywhere. Her eyes met mine.

I said, "Why did you say you'd Go with me?"

She made a face like this might have been the stupidest question she'd ever been asked.

She said, "Why'd you ask me?"

I nodded. Must be a family thing, this question-for-a-question deal.

Going back up the hallway, I heard the door behind me close. A sound that ended, in the silence, with a deafening click.

AT NIGHT the streetlight beyond our rock garden streamed through the magnolia before my bedroom window, silvering the headboard of my bed, darkening the carved lines of a high-masted ship that rode the sea. Lying awake, staring at that ship, at the sea, I would wonder about him, ensconced in his pondside house, his bower of ragged cedars. Here was the fabled stranger, a man starkly apart, and as wholly other to me as any. Still, I came to imagine him—in the silence and solitude of the little house, pausing to listen to the squirrels scrabble over the shingles, or in that johnboat, gliding out from beneath the willows, resting the paddle handle across his thigh, watching the dripping from the blade—having some reason in that moment to recall, to imagine, me.

At his age he would know so much more than I did, so much more about us all, including me. But he would not know, would not remember, everything. He would not *be* me. So he would have his questions. As I had mine for him. Like: *What on earth do you do all day?* and *Is there something wrong with you?*

I STEPPED OFF the porch into the Barrys' front yard, amid the booming of the cicadas and the frogs and the locusts, feeling terrifically free and interested in the rest of my life. Here I am, world.

But there was little light left.

And so many others to find.

Damn this gathering dark.

Through it now Zeke and John Dixon came running around the corner of the house, Zeke hollering, "Stop it, I quit!" John Dixon hollering, *"Ahh-gll-ahh-gll!"* and legally blind Lance Reynolds, advantaged by long familiarity with the playing conditions, right on their behind, helicoptering the crushed squirrel by the tail.

I said, "Lance, buddy, put that down and y'all come on."

Maybe it was something in my voice. All three stopped. Lance lowered the squirrel.

John Dixon said, "Where we going?"

I said, "Everybody's meeting at the bridge."

Lance said, "Yeah, I heard about that," and while we waited for him to go put the squirrel in his mailbox, these words of his stirred my hopes—I couldn't say who all had heard, who all I might find there—and on Lance's return I started us down the street, double-time.

Porch lights were coming on.

Zeke said, "Why's everybody meeting at the bridge?"

As of course he would.

I clapped him warmly on the shoulder, kept us in stride.

I said, "We're heading to the Angel's Pond. To visit poor Cletus."

Zeke said, "You are not for real."

John Dixon said, "Poor who?"

Lance said, "Isn't it getting dark?"

I'd had to take Zeke by the arm.

He said, "There *ain't* no Cletus!"

And how could I answer that?

I glanced up a street soon to vanish into night.

Faith, boy. Faith!

I said, "Reckon we'll find out, won't we."

DREAM ABOUT Bailey Peterson: I am walking the highway in a high night wind, heading out of town, when his parents pull to the shoulder in a moon-white limousine. Out steps Bailey, looking like he did when we were in junior high. Red plaid button-down. Swooped blond bangs. He doesn't speak, but there he stands, every bit as alive as I am.

THE LAST TIME I SAW Mr. Peterson was maybe thirty years ago, at a shoe store down in Jackson, a year or so after Bailey died. It was a sudden, round-an-aisle kind of meeting, and initially I panicked: I had not attended the funeral, or seen any of his family since hearing of Bailey's death, and I had no idea how to handle this, no idea what to say, and no chance to hide. Mr. Peterson, God bless him, did not flinch. He was as noble as ever, and for that moment pulled me up with him. After warmly shaking my hand and asking after my family, he straightaway mentioned Bailey, how badly they missed him, how hard it was. This still seems incredible to me, that he should be able to say it. I mean, he actually said something like "Oh, Michael, we miss that boy . . . ." Words that, to look at them, strike me as profanely inadequate. But in the way he said them that day, in the place he said them from, Mr. Peterson managed to acknowledge every whit of their inadequacy while, at the same time, claiming a faith in saying them anyway—and in so doing, won out. For both of us.

Bailey and I were never close, but he once told me of a talk his father had with him about drinking. We were in the ninth grade (paired up in French to build a paperboard model of the Eiffel Tower), and I don't know that either of us had yet begun to think much about drinking, so I'm not sure how the subject came up. But Mr. Peterson had told Bailey he expected Bailey would soon want to try drinking beer, and even getting drunk, as teenage boys are wont to do. All he asked was that Bailey not do it while riding around in a car. He would rather him do it—and this I had to have Bailey repeat—at home. I don't know whether Bailey ever took him up on that, and I have difficulty picturing just how they would have managed it.

In any event, Bailey died as a freshman in college, when one Friday night his car left the pavement of a particularly lonesome stretch of Mississippi back road, found a ditch, and slammed into a culvert. I remember my relief on hearing he had not been drinking. Apparently he'd simply fallen asleep on a late run home from Sewanee. From what I heard, he was upset over a girl and wanted to be with his family. But here is what holds me: he sat out there by himself, dead, until Sunday morning. What in this world can it mean that two times the night pulled back and the sun rose on him, that not once but twice its promise trickled through the spidered windshield onto a still unblinking face?

IN COLLEGE, sometime after seeing Mr. Peterson in the shoe store, I bought a small black hardcover of the 1979 Episcopal *Book of Common Prayer*. Its boards now show at the corners. In it I have marked a prayer in the service for compline, attributed to St. Augustine:

> *Keep watch, dear Lord, with those who work, or watch, or weep this night, and give your angels charge over those who sleep. Tend the sick, Lord Christ; give rest to the weary, bless the dying, soothe the suffering, pity the afflicted, shield the joyous; and all for your love's sake. Amen.*

At times I've had it memorized. But there are lots of folks in there to remember, and often when I try to recall it, I can tell by the wronged rhythm of its music some-thing is out of order, or I am leaving somebody out, and not infrequently I forget even how to start it. So the book remains at hand.

SOME MORNING I will come walking back up from the pond, or glance out the bedroom window, and spot a dutiful neighborhood father striding across the open grass of the hillside, or maybe a deputy's cruiser creeping into view through the trees from the water tower, and instead of going out to meet whoever it is, I will loiter somewhere in the back of the house, awaiting the sharp, one-knuckle knock on the frame of the screen door, then go calmly, straight-faced, up the narrow hallway toward where he stands, hands on his hips, done with survey-ing the dirty white clapboard, the surrounding cedars, his smile now strained with trying to peer through the filthy screen, as though down the long, dim shaft of a well, until at last he sees my face and figure come floating slowly up out of the darkness, my hand rise to unlatch the screen, cueing him to reach for and find the prompt, resonant voice of leadership and community:

"How you doing? I don't believe we've met before . . . ."

This evening, I estimate I could not handle it.

Oh, God, make speed to save me from it. And from this dimming of the day, the incessant thunder of the frogs, the infernal *ratchi-chit, ratchi-chit* of the bugs, the high treelines darkening against the sky, towering me in.

But—what is this?

In the deepening dusk, from the purple of the woods toward the neighborhood, spilling visible upon the open grass: a stream of shapes. A surging, motley parade my way in the afterglow.

## ACKNOWLEDGMENTS

I am deeply grateful to and for the friends who read and commented on earlier drafts: Shelia H, Tom P, John E, Jim B, Michael P, Claire H, Harvey K, Sara M-B, David N, Christian K, Maria H, Eric J, Porter S, Kathy P, Karen M, and Ted W.

And special thanks to the following:

the Speranza Foundation, Wedgwood Circle, the Community of Writers at Squaw Valley, and Laity Lodge, for refuge;
my Greensboro gang, forever in my heart;
my mother and father, always;
Bud and Sissy, dear ones;
Dr. Laura H, angel in the wilderness;
Edmond, who changed everything;
Nate and Jack, my joy, my believers; and
Claire—for more than can be said.